Advance Praise for

WAKING THE ANCIENTS

"Gail Holstein's *Waking the Ancients* is a fast-paced tale of our times in a timeless setting."

—Bruce Berger, poet, pianist, naturalist; winner of Western States Book Award and Colorado Book Author Award for *The Telling Distance*

"*Waking the Ancients* is a novel you won't put down, a suspenseful adventure whose characters get trapped in a nightmare . . . high in the cliff wilderness of Arizona. Gail Holstein fascinates with her knowledge of the mysterious Mogollon, cliff dwellers who disappeared hundreds of years ago . . . in a plot filled with tension, then escalating terror. Think Hillerman mixed with Mary Higgins Clark. I highly recommend!"

—Barbara Bartocci, popular, multi-book author of *Nobody's Child Anymore* and others

"A page turner . . . Only Gail Holstein could write about such diametrically opposed life styles and bring them both to life."

—David Sontag, screenwriter, producer, Director, Writing for the Screen and Stage Program, The University of North Carolina at Chapel Hill

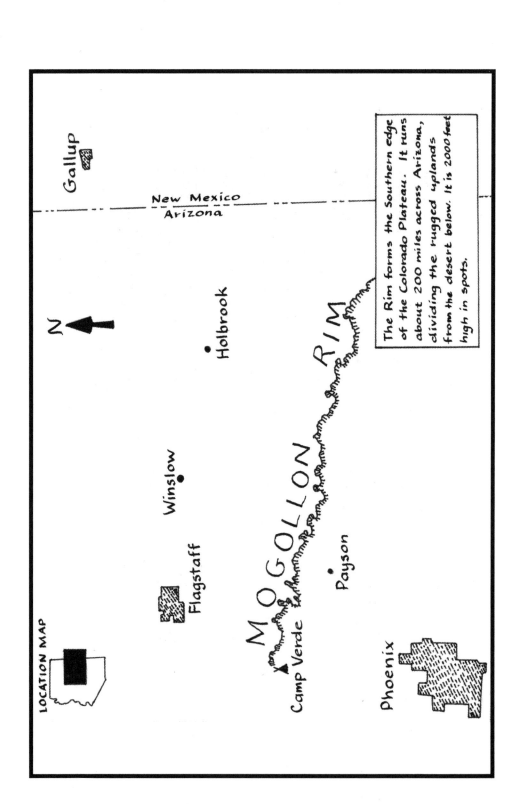

LOCATION MAP

N

Gallup

New Mexico
Arizona

Holbrook

Winslow

Flagstaff

MOGOLLON

Camp Verde

RIM

Payson

Phoenix

The Rim forms the Southern edge of the Colorado Plateau. It runs about 200 miles across Arizona, dividing the rugged uplands from the desert below. It is 2000 feet high in spots.

All the best —
enjoy your adventures —
Gail Holstein

WAKING
THE ANCIENTS

A Novel of the Mogollon Rim

GAIL WANMAN HOLSTEIN

Thundercloud Books
ASPEN, COLORADO

This book is a work of fiction. Names, characters, places and events are products of the author's imagination or are used fictitiously. Any resemblance to actual events, locations or persons, living or deceased, is purely coincidental. We assume no responsibility for errors, inaccuracies, omissions, or any inconsistency herein.

First printing 2003

Photos: Global Fitness Adventures
        Matthew Holstein

ISBN 0-9740806-3-2
LCCN 2003105799

ATTENTION CORPORATIONS, UNIVERSITIES, COLLEGES, AND PROFESSIONAL ORGANIZATIONS: Quantity discounts are available on bulk purchases of this book for educational or gift purposes, or as premiums for increasing magazine subscriptions or renewals. Special books or book excerpts can also be created to fit specific needs. For information, please contact Thundercloud Books, P.O. Box 97, Aspen, CO 81612. Phone (970) 925-1588.

Thanks!

A novel has many parents. It's the baby in a family of characters, real and imaginary. I'd like to thank some of the real ones for helping bring this book into the world.

On a camping trip, I watched my husband Phil gather sage for a smudging ceremony. Suddenly, I had the plot for *Waking the Ancients*. His decades-long enthusiasm for prehistoric art and culture was the original seed.

A legion of first-rate friends offered suggestions for the book. Going beyond the call were Claire McDougall, Samantha Sandler, Lynne Arundale, Sandra Wanman, Ellen Hunt, Steven Alldredge, and Carol Bell, who big-heartedly critiqued the funky early drafts.

My excellent daughter, Laurel Tesoro, was relentless in her encouragement, from conception to term. My excellent son, Matt Holstein, concurred as to the brilliance of the project and also took pictures. Joyce Meredith gamely drew the map. Barbara Bartocci and Kristina Hurrell were generous helpers, spiritual guides, and cheerleaders. Our competent midwife was About Books, Inc.

"…a strange freak of nature, a mountain canted on one side."

— *Captain John G. Bourke,*
aide to General George Crook,
describing the Mogollon Rim in 1871

"Life is short; death is long."

—*Unknown*

<u>Chapter 1</u>

As if a hand were shaking her, Leah gasped and sat up. The room was dark and silent. Then she remembered: this was her new bed, her new room. The clock's red digits flickered like fires across a canyon. Five thirty-eight.

She let her breath out. "Branson?"

A slit of light shone under the bathroom door. So he was home from the pueblos, as promised. She snuggled back under the puffy quilt, loving the way he showered and came to bed warm, to melt the glacier of loneliness she'd slept on since he left.

Moments later she stiffened again, as a high-pitched whistle streamed through the bungalow. She sensed Branson's quiet step, pausing at each door: kitchen, laundry, kids' rooms. And she smelled pot.

His naked figure filled the doorway, the hairs on his arms lit against the dawn. Tendrils of smoke curled up from a small bowl in his hand. He fanned the wisps with a feather, then blew his whistle. He stepped around their bed, affording her a welcome view of his mountain-biker buttocks.

She touched his thigh. "Branson?"

"Almost finished."

He was up to some wacko Anasazi thing again. Leah wanted him to stop it, come to her, and do what he did so well.

He slipped out of the room, leaving an herbal trail on the air. When he returned, he slid in behind her and ran his hand up her back. A two-day scratch of whiskers tickled her neck; his lips found her ear.

"The return of the native," she said.

He laughed. "'Home is the hunter, from the hill.'"

"'Home is the hunter,' to his ticky-tacky box in Phoenix."

"To his very patient wife." His fingers dug softly into her shoulder blades. "Sorry I'm late."

1

She rolled over toward him. "Don't worry, you'll pay." She took a long sniff of him. "You smell like grass."

"It's sage, for cleansing."

"Cleansing. And the whistle?"

"Eagle bone. Calls the spirits." He massaged her breasts, crawled on top of her. His chest was heavy on hers, his knee separating her legs.

"And when will the spirits come?"

"They're here now."

"I don't see any spirits."

He wrapped his arms beneath her and pulled her hips to him. "They're here."

The street light outside switched off: six o'clock, as programmed, every morning in September. The sun lurked behind the identical house across the street. Leah grabbed a handful of Branson's dark hair and pulled his head to her chest. "We don't need spirits," she whispered.

He paused, as if listening. "Too late. We've got them."

While Branson slept, Leah made breakfast for her daughter, then turned her loose to roam the neighborhood of phony-adobe houses. All of them, including theirs, looked like countless other houses in Phoenix, as if they'd been packaged on assembly belts.

Eight-year-old Alissa danced, rather than walked, flipping her dark bangs back from her startling blue eyes. "I'm gonna get a pink bike, a pink bike," she sang.

Phoenix was a great adventure for Alissa. She didn't notice the step down from their Philadelphia lifestyle, didn't care that the new bike would be coming from a swap meet. Leah wondered how long until Alissa figured out secondhand bicycles were not hip, that a best friend whose father was in prison wasn't a social asset, and that her own father was pretty weird himself.

She boiled water in a saucepan and used a paper towel to filter the coffee. At least Branson hadn't outlawed paper towels—not yet, anyway. She woke their son, who slept beneath a wall of sports posters, a basketball sharing his pillow.

"Hey, Geoffrey. You're wasting a perfectly acceptable Saturday morning."

He pushed his pale-flame hair, the same color as Leah's, off his forehead. "Dad make it back?"

"Middle of the night."

"Cool."

"We're taking Alissa to the swap meet to get her bike."

"Isn't Jim coming over?"

Leah made her voice expressionless, as she practiced doing when Howlin' Jim's name came up. "Dad's had enough Jim for a while. Anyway, Saturday is family day."

Geoffrey went outdoors to shoot hoops with his tribe of pre-adolescents. Leah drank her coffee and stared out the cookie-cutter front window.

Phoenix is no place for human beings, she thought. Yet Phoenix was where they lived now, like space colonists in a bright, thin-aired metropolis, dependent on captured rivers for life support. And if the sprawling city weren't unnatural enough, there was Howlin' Jim, and the spirits, and the desert—all vying for her husband's attention.

I want to go back to Philadelphia. It was the first time she'd allowed herself to think it. For five months she'd "appreciated" Phoenix, "forgotten" her old life, the tennis club, her garden, their colonial house on a street of towering maples. The only large plant here was the saguaro cactus, and who could love a fifteen-foot Gumby? She sighed: *Philadelphia.*

Branson's bowl sat on the shelf, eagle feather beside it, a couple of beads tied to the shaft. She sniffed the sagebrush ashes.

"Cleansing." It was a flat statement. She could stay neutral; she could stay hinged. Lately she was almost as unpredictable as Branson, strung between worshipping him and wanting to punch his handsome jaw. When he talked about spirits, she felt the ground beneath them keep shifting.

She picked up the eagle feather and took a couple of hops. "Me chief Smoke-in-the-Face. Me call spirits, cleanse your lousy little house." She lifted the bone whistle to her lips.

"Put that down." It was Branson, behind her.

He was watching from the door of their room, arms crossed, face in silent-Indian mode. She set the whistle on the shelf.

"Don't touch those again."

"Branson, stop being a jerk."

He crossed the room in three steps and grabbed her forearms. "And don't joke about the ancients."

Their sixteen years together seemed to vanish into the Arizona sky. He had never strong-armed her like that, back in Philadelphia. What was wrong with him? With them?

"Let go of my arm."

He turned and strode back to the bedroom.

To still her trembling, she stumbled to the washer and made a stab at sorting the laundry. But her vision kept blurring.

If she had refused to come to Phoenix, Branson would have come by himself. These days, if she tried to joke or tease or laugh, he turned stone serious. He left her and the kids for days at a time, saying his "spirit" was with the Anasazi—a race of people who disappeared six hundred years ago.

I want him normal. That's all. I want us normal. A sour lump of resentment settled in her stomach. "Damn it, Branson," she muttered. Wiping her face on Alissa's little shirt, she stuffed the kids' clothes into the washer and listened as the machine filled.

Yet there was the smell of him on her skin, from their lovemaking just hours before. How sweet he had been. How well he knew what she needed.

Branson stood behind her, wearing jeans but still shirtless. He pulled her to him with his sinewy arms. She held her breath.

"Sorry," he said.

"I can't take this, Branson."

He turned her toward him, pressing her face into the dark hairs of his chest. "You won't be taking it much longer."

"What're you talking about?"

"You'll know, soon enough."

"Branson, stop being mysterious. You leave for three days and come back talking in riddles. It's always the goddamned spirits. It's always your goddamned Jim."

"Quiet, Leah." He kissed her forehead.

She squirmed away. "Don't tell me to be quiet. I'm sick of being quiet. I'm sick of the ancients."

"Shh." He held her, kneading her shoulders and nuzzling her neck, until she loosened. He lifted her up onto the dryer, pressing her into the pile of clothes.

She cursed herself for surrendering, even as she wrapped her legs around his narrow waist and slipped back into the warmth she craved. It was easier like this. Her arms found their way to his neck, her lips to his lips. "Stay," she said. At that moment, she wouldn't mind spending the day on top of the dryer, if he would just be there with her.

4

Leah felt Branson shift his weight, then stand up. She opened her eyes and peered over his shoulder. Howlin' Jim, the last person she wanted to see, was in the living room.

She yanked her shirt down. "Do you ever knock? Use the doorbell?"

Jim didn't move. "Leah," he said with a nod that both acknowledged and dismissed her. In moccasins and a pony tail, he stood with arms crossed over his skinny chest, as if he were waiting for a rainstorm in the desert.

Branson was already in the living room. The men shook hands with a cornball elbow grip out of a noble-savage movie. "I'll be ready in a minute," Branson said, and disappeared into the bedroom.

"Hey," she called after him, once again wretched as a refugee. "What about the swap meet?"

Jim said, "I have some things to show Branson."

"Yeah, well, so do I. And he promised Alissa."

"His mistake."

Jim's long hair, once dark, was sprinkled with gray. His moustache covered his top lip, making it difficult to read his expression. His eyes, even lighter than Alissa's, were a pair of marbles set in his sun-hardened face. Around his neck hung a leather thong with beads and small animal parts. Leah had watched with dread as this disturbing man moved into Branson's life.

Branson came into the room, wearing a cotton shirt tucked in neatly. Apart from the beaded leather string around his neck, he resembled the civilized man he used to be.

"Let's go."

Leah was dangling over a void, losing her grip. "Branson," she squeaked. "The bike. Alissa."

Branson's sharp features twisted in conflict. He appeared about to capitulate; but instead, he handed her his wallet. "You take Alissa. Buy her any bike she wants."

"But you're supposed to see it. That's the whole point."

"I'll see it later. Car key's on the dresser. Jim, ready?"

They slipped out the back door, onto the little patio surrounded by a fake-adobe wall. A moment later, they moved past the side of the house and crossed the front yard.

Jim's sand-colored eighties-vintage International Travelall lurked at the curb. His dog Chaco, same color as the car, waited on the unnatural green lawn. When he saw them, he leapt through the window and took his place in the back. After a couple of false starts, the car lumbered down the street, scattering kids.

Leah picked up Branson's bowl, hesitating just a moment before flinging it. "Screw you, Howlin' Jim! Screw you, ancients!" The bowl whacked into the hollow-core front door, leaving a dent, and thumped unbroken to the carpet.

She trudged back to the laundry room, emptied the washer. Branson's grubby jeans and T-shirt lay on the hamper. They were smeared with grease, rather than stuck with twigs and smelling of campfire, as they usually were when he'd been out with Jim.

He hadn't mentioned having car trouble. But then, he didn't mention much of anything these days. Greasy jeans hardly qualified as a topic of conversation, when spirits and loonies are stealing your husband.

Chapter 2

While Leah unloaded the little bike, Alissa jumped out of the Volvo and leapt into her father's arms. He tossed her high, making her squeal. She squirmed down and picked up the bike.

"Watch me, Dad! I can already ride it!" She sped away to circle a manhole.

The new bike attracted the children from the surrounding houses. Geoffrey, cool as only twelve-year-boys can be cool, passed his basketball to a buddy and ambled over, hands in the pockets of his droopy pants, sprigs of carroty hair poking out beneath his backward-facing baseball cap. Branson gave him a manly upper-body hug.

"Geoffrey, look!" Alissa called. "No hands!"

Though Leah was still angry, she watched her little family, all gathered together on a normal street in front of their normal American house, and didn't want to be a grinch. Besides, Branson flashed her his rare smile. His straight teeth and smoky eyes drew her in, as they always did.

"Hey," Branson called. "Who wants to go camping?"

"Yeah!" Alissa jumped off the bike, then looked at it with regret.

"Your bike will be here when you get back."

"Yeah, well, okay."

"So let's move."

Alissa ran to get her Barbies ready for the trip. Geoffrey tossed the basketball a few more times, then helped his father load the car.

If it were always like this, I could stand living here, Leah thought. *The kids, the nice daddy, the picnics and camping.*

The afternoon was glaring hot as they drove to the supermarket. She glanced at Geoffrey, who had also tied a thin leather strap around his neck.

"What's that thing?"

"Nothing."

"Branson, what's he wearing?"

Branson squeezed Leah's thigh and pulled her toward him on the seat. "Hey, come here, squaw."

"Dad," Alissa piped from the back seat. "Mom's supposed to stay in her seat with her belt on. It's the law."

"The law. I forgot." Branson laughed, the way he did whenever he was pulling some marginal maneuver, his outlaw laugh. He turned the Volvo into the acres-wide parking lot. "Okay, troops, in and out of this boorgie store in ten minutes."

"Boorgie?" said Leah. "Is that a new word?"

"Yeah. Like bourgeois. You know I hate this scene."

"We have to eat, Branson. Which means the supermarket, unless you're going to shoot our dinner for us."

Branson didn't laugh.

Leah rolled her cart through the bright, frigid aisles, picking out steaks and chips and even chocolate cookies—things Branson disapproved of since Phoenix—defying him to nix them. He glanced at the cart and said nothing.

As they waited at the counter for the manager's check approval, the ruddy-faced clerk patted his belly and studied Branson's driver's license.

"Branson Ellis. Pennsylvania, eh? I don't suppose you'd be one of the Philadelphia Ellises?"

Leah liked the friendliness of Arizonans. "As a matter of fact—"

"Nope," said Branson.

"'Cause, you know, Ellis Equipment's got their headquarters in Philadelphia. I'm from western P.A. myself. Had a farm there. I grew up with Ellis machinery. We never bought anything but an Ellis. Threshers, seeders, even the lawn mower was an Ellis, I remember."

"Where's that flunky with my check?"

Leah gaped at Branson, shocked by his rudeness.

The clerk didn't notice. "I'm a transplant myself. Guess you hardly ever meet a real native out here, do you? That Ellis equipment, though, that was the best. I can remember—"

Branson picked up the grocery bags. "We're going."

"Sir? The manager's coming with your check. Sir?"

Branson strode out of the store, with Leah and the kids struggling to keep up, Alissa tripping over her shoelace and Geoffrey managing to speed up his slouch. They tossed the groceries on top of the sleeping bags and clambered in. Branson threw the car into reverse and screeched out of the parking lot.

Not until they'd cleared Apache Junction—just another part of Phoenix despite its historic name—did Leah break the silence.

"I can't believe you did that."

"Believe it."

"Were the ancients impolite?"

"They didn't put up with boorgie crap."

"It's just common courtesy, Branson. He was making conversation."

"He was prattling. Wasting his words, not a thought in his head. I don't have time for those people anymore."

Leah rode in silence, watching as the subdivisions became sparse, the emptiness of the desert obvious. Branson had a point; the clerk was a yammering immigrant, claiming his few square feet of living space in a harsh landscape, where humans wouldn't survive without air-conditioned cars and buildings.

Still, who was Branson, or she, to judge? How were they any different from the clerk?

She looked at his face, the face she never used to tire of watching. His brow was set in a thoughtful scowl. Even more than in Philadelphia, these days he seemed to hear something she did not. Even more than before, Leah was only a part of his life, whereas he was the whole of hers.

"You look like an Indian," she said.

"I'll take that as a compliment."

"Where are we going?"

"You'll like this camp. Tomorrow we'll hike to a ruin that was excavated in the forties, where you can see the layout of the rooms. The kiva's partly reconstructed."

"A veritable Disney World of the ancients."

"Well, it's a good intro."

"Haven't we had enough intro, with all the museums you've taken us to? Aren't we ready for the advanced class?"

He smiled. "Soon."

Branson, stay with us. Stay in our world.

They turned north toward Canyon Lake. The road narrowed as they climbed from suburb to desert to dun-colored hills. The air was fresh and light, the arc of the sun lower now, as September pried open the sauna of summer. They cruised through Tortilla Flats, with its cutesy western storefronts and wooden sidewalk. Alissa bounced in the back seat. Geoffrey fingered his fetish necklace and took in the cactus and sand and hills. Leah kept watching Branson.

"Hey, Anasazi Man."

"Speak, squaw." Branson grinned.

"Since when is it a crime to be a Philadelphia Ellis?"

His smile vanished. "It always has been. I only recently figured it out."

"Excuse me? Ellis Equipment has provided us an extremely decent living."

"Yeah.

"Ellis makes it possible never to have to work again."

"Let's not get into it, Leah. We're almost there."

He pulled off the blacktop and steered a path across the hard-packed desert, past skittering lizards and saguaro cactus making frozen gestures against the evening sky. He was following an arroyo, a desert sand river that was always dry, except when flooded. Far behind, Phoenix glowed like a carnival.

Twenty feet from the rim of a wide canyon, Branson stopped the car. On the opposite side, hundreds of feet away, rounded rocks hunched like piles of soft ice cream.

"Wow," Geoffrey said. He and Alissa ran to the edge to yell, delighted with their echoes.

"We have to walk down." Branson shouldered his big pack and disappeared over the side of the cliff, as casually as he would stroll through his own house. Leah and the kids struggled into their packs and trudged after him.

The campsite, about half a mile down, was a sandy shelf beneath a spectacular, buff-colored wall. The glow of Phoenix was no longer visible, but the moon, almost full, rose behind the pinnacles and mounds on the opposite side.

Leah dropped her pack and sleeping bag into the sand. "So, do you come here with Howlin' Jim?"

"Look, Leah, you wanted me to bring you."

"Just answer my question."

"Jim knows this place, yes."

"You and Jim come here to commune with the ancients?"

"Yes." Branson was re-setting the blackened rocks of a much-used fire ring.

"I guess we should feel honored."

Branson pulled his knife out and cleaned it on the rough fabric of his jeans. "It's just a great spot. I thought you'd like it."

"There aren't any ancients here." Leah started unpacking food.

"There are."

"Whatever. At least Jim's giving us the night off."

The kids scouted for twigs and sticks; Branson started a fire. The flames splashed the wall behind them hot orange, and the children's movements cast frantic shadows. Leah spread the sleeping bags in the sand—kids' near the fire, parents' ragged doublewide in the shadow of a creosote bush.

After dinner they sat and watched the flames take the wood. Leah, relaxed now, said, "Fire gazing. The Anasazi got some things right."

Branson warmed to his favorite topic. "Actually, the ancients who lived here weren't Anasazi, but Hohokam. The Anasazi lived farther north. Between the Anasazi and the Hohokam were the Mogollon."

"Mogo-yawn?" Alissa laughed.

"That's right. They lived on the Mogollon Rim."

"How come they didn't fall off?"

Branson smiled. "The Rim's a huge cliff up by Flagstaff. It's a quarter of a mile high, two hundred miles from west to east. The Mogollon people lived in houses in the cliff, and in the forest below."

Alissa frowned. "How do we know their name was Mogo-yawn?"

"We don't know. That name was given to them later by the Spanish. 'Anasazi' means 'enemy ancestor' in Navajo. 'Hohokam' means 'those who have gone' in Pima. Got all that, Liss? There'll be a quiz."

"Anasazi, Ho-ho-kam, Mogo-yawn."

"Your dad's become quite the expert," Leah said.

Geoffrey turned a small log over with the heel of his sneaker. "Howlin' Jim knows more than Dad."

"Please, Geoffrey, just for tonight, consider your father the source of all wisdom."

Branson smiled. "In ancient days, a man my age was very old."

Alissa giggled and climbed into her father's lap. "You are very old, in these days."

"Now listen here, pipsqueak. The ancients treated their elders with respect."

"That's because they were gonna die soon, and they didn't want them to come back and haunt 'em," said Alissa. "We studied it in school."

"Doofus," Geoffrey said. "They respected old people for their wisdom."

"That's right," said Branson. "If you lived to be old, you had a lot going for you."

Leah tossed a piece of saguaro bark over the cliff. "Oh, right. Crumbling bones, rotten teeth, stomach parasites. No medicine, just voodoo."

"Magic and medicine were the same word, actually."

"Well, I'm glad they're different words today." Leah stretched. "Who wants another marshmallow?"

Alissa sat up. "They buried people inside their houses."

"Yep."

"Gross."

Geoffrey finished off his marshmallow and laid the stick next to the fire. "Is there a burial where we're hiking tomorrow?"

"Yes. But the scientists took away all the bones and artifacts."

Geoffrey stood, mumbled good night, and wandered over to his sleeping bag. Leah watched their daughter fall asleep in Branson's arms. Branson stood up and slid her into her sleeping bag.

Leah wrapped her arms around Branson's waist. His taut stomach muscles never failed to interest her. "Time to tuck me in, too."

He wasn't listening to her. His head was cocked toward the canyon.

"What?" she said. "You're not hearing spirits."

"Maybe not."

"Branson, don't start that."

His arm on her shoulder, he walked her to the lip of the canyon. The void below them was dark and alive. Leah heard nothing but the rustle of breeze in the creosote bush, the whisper of tiny scavengers making a banquet of their leavings. Branson froze, listening.

"What?" she said.

"It's the ancients. They never go."

Leah awoke in a blast of sunlight. Branson was gone. Large paw prints surrounded their sleeping bag.

She leapt out of the bag and ran to the children. Seeing them both asleep, she sat on the log and breathed, to quiet the pounding in her chest.

She pulled off her T-shirt and dipped her washcloth into the pan of water, remembering to enjoy the spectacular view, the fresh morning air. Branson had said the ruin was on the other side of the steep canyon; she couldn't imagine how they'd get there. She scrubbed her face and armpits, then combed her hair and pulled it into a ponytail.

The sound of a footstep came from the trail. A large dog bounded into the campsite.

"Chaco!"

Howlin' Jim stepped onto the sand. His sinewy chest was painted with three yellow circles, and blue streaks extended from his eyes to his chin. He held a long, slender bow; a hand-stitched quiver was slung across his back, held by a woven rope across his chest.

Leah grabbed her shirt and yanked it on over her head. "What the hell are you doing here?"

"Came to get the boy."

"You're out of your mind." Leah backed up, getting between Jim and the children.

"Branson sent me. He's already halfway down the canyon. You and the girl can take the short way, and we'll meet you at the ruin."

"No way, Jim."

Jim nudged her aside and knelt beside Geoffrey. "Kaibito, wake up. Men's walkabout day." He stared back at Leah, his face impassive, his leathery skin wrinkled under the blue paint.

Geoffrey wiggled out of his bag and looked across the canyon, then sat to put his sneakers on. "What about Mom and Alissa?"

"We'll leave signs for them. Your father's gone ahead to build the first cairn at the bottom. We'll all meet on the other side."

"Cool."

"Just a minute, Geoffrey." Leah took him by the shoulders. "What's so damned cool about it? This is a family hike. You're going with us."

"He'll be with his father," Jim said.

"Mom." Geoffrey stepped away from Leah's grasp. "Please?"

Leah felt herself weaken. "Take something to eat." She shoved a chunk of bread, some leftover steak, and an apple into his pack. "Here, take water. Hold still, Geoffrey." She smeared his face with sunblock.

Geoffrey endured his mother's attention and even muttered thanks. But he was eager to turn and follow Jim over the sandy shelf.

Leah, convinced she'd never see him again, ran to the edge. They were already far down the steep side, walking fast, single file, Jim in the lead. They ducked around a boulder. Ninety seconds later she saw them again, farther down, trudging across a debris-strewn wash. She watched her son disappear.

Chapter 3

"Damn, damn," Leah muttered. She and Alissa were picking their way along the canyon wall.

Geoffrey and Jim had seemed to amble down with ease, but she could barely find footholds. Every step set pebbles careening down the side.

I've had it. We're going back. Not five more minutes of this, I swear it.

"You scared, Mom?" Alissa called.

"No, silly, of course not. What makes you think that?"

"'Cause you're saying curse words."

"I am not."

"Damn?'"

"Don't be a smarty."

"Want me to lead?"

"Absolutely not. Look down there. I think that's the cairn."

Alissa scrambled around her mother and headed straight down the cliff. She reached the bottom of the canyon and was sitting by the rock marker, drawing with a twig in the sand and humming, when Leah arrived.

"Hey, mountain goat." Leah sat down and pulled out her water bottle. "You're making me look like a wimp."

"But you're not, Mom. Most old people wouldn't do that climb."

"Thanks. I appreciate that." She surveyed the narrow floor of the canyon and let her eyes trail up the implausibly steep side they'd just descended; the other side looked unclimbable. "Well, now what?"

"Looky. I found this on the cairn." Alissa handed her a turquoise nugget, crudely carved into a canine shape—wolf or coyote.

"Huh. Howlin' Jim's talisman." She slipped it into the pocket of her shorts. "Okay, Liss, you ready to move?"

The sun climbed higher, bringing out sweat under the shoulder straps of Leah's pack. They followed the trail along the dry streambed until it stopped at the canyon wall, a solid expanse of gray stone, ten stories straight up. Leah felt like a bug in a jar. How the hell were they supposed to climb that?

He said there'd be signs.

She told Alissa to wait in the shadow of a big boulder, then began to pace. There were only two possible directions: upstream and downstream. A waist-high ledge, three inches wide, ran along the wall like the wainscoting in their old Philadelphia house. Could Jim mean for them to climb up on it?

A dot of bright green caught her eye. Half buried in the sand of the ledge was another bit of turquoise, no longer than her fingernail. It, too, was carved into an animal. Directly above the nugget was a long, vertical slit. She ran her hand up as far as she could reach, felt the slit widen. She had just enough strength to pull herself up on the ledge and peer in. It was a slot canyon, expanding as it went up.

Relieved, irritated, Leah jumped down and called Alissa.

"You're kidding, right, Mom?" Alissa said, squinting up at the slit.

"I wish. Here, let me boost you."

"What if we just went back to camp?"

"And let them think we're losers?"

"You're right." Alissa stood in her mother's laced fingers and vaulted onto the ledge. "Hey, this doesn't look so hard." She squeezed herself into the slot.

The fissure was convoluted, smoothed by eons of water and wind. They wedged themselves into it, crawled beneath overhangs, scooted across surfaces coated in centuries of bat guano. As they worked their way upward, Alissa kept her eyes on the sliver of sky above the broadening crack.

"I bet they're waiting for us right up top," she panted.

They hauled themselves out of the slot, like swimmers from a pool, onto a wide, sun-battered plain. There was nothing there.

"Mom?"

What the hell.

But Leah couldn't show her fear. "Hey, it's lunchtime!" She sat in the sand and started digging in her pack.

"Where are they?"

"Oh, probably out chasing rabbits. Why don't you crawl down out of the sun, and I'll hand you your sandwich."

Alissa surveyed the flat landscape, with its limited options. "Okay. Just like the queen, huh?"

"Yeah. Peanut butter, your majesty?"

The little girl munched her sandwich, confident Leah had everything figured out, and fell asleep on the cool sand beneath the rocky overhang.

Leah walked to the edge of the chasm. Far away, through a dirty haze, shimmered the other wall of the canyon, where they'd spent the night. There was no way to retrace their steps now. Even if they made it down the slot, they wouldn't find the cairn and get up the crumbly cliff before dark.

The desert had never seemed so vast. A city of two million people simmered just beyond the horizon, but it might as well be on another planet. Leah's knees went weak; she sat on the harsh sand and let the tears come.

Maybe those weren't even Howlin' Jim's turquoises. Maybe some poor, lost, prehistoric Indian left them, hundreds of years ago, and I just followed them. I'm a fool.

For the first time, Leah considered that Branson might be more than just "strange." There had been plenty of red flags. His silence, his indifference to her, his hostility toward his family back east, his disappearances—why hadn't she put it together? Back in Philadelphia, he'd morphed from carefree, rich guy, always up for a party or a camping trip, into Mister Silent Indian. Spent evenings with a book instead of a beer, listening to something beyond her earshot. Why hadn't she taken him to a shrink, the minute he started talking about ghosts and Anasazis?

Tears dripped onto her T-shirt. She wiped her nose on her arm. In Phoenix, where he'd been pulled as if by an invisible rope, Branson collected none of the usual kachinas, baskets, fetishes, or pots—none of the things he studied in museums and books. Nor would he let her furnish their crummy rented house—"no more consumer crap," he said. He no longer personally owned anything he hadn't found or made. All he had was his medicine bundle, a sinew-wrapped rag that contained spooky, grimy things.

And there was Howlin' Jim. Jim was a creep. A smart creep, one who spoke to Branson in ways Leah could not, who connected him with the shadow world—as if such a world existed.

She had run out of tears. She stood and went to Alissa's cool napping spot. The girl's eyelids twitched as she slept, but she was smiling.

At least Branson had a passion. At least he had friend here.

Which was more than she could say for herself. She missed BJ. What would BJ say, BJ with her cute figure and her Donna Karan suits and her great career, if she could see Leah now?

"Aw, hell," she'd say. "Have a beer. Tell me what's on your beautiful mind."

BJ would understand.

I'll call her as soon as we get home. I'll just tell her everything. She pictured BJ at her desk, her secretary holding off important clients so BJ could listen to Leah cry and blow her nose. "You're my job, too, honey," she'd say. "I owe you. You've helped keep me sane plenty of times."

But we could die here. I may never get to call her.

Maybe Jim was trying to get rid of her. Maybe he'd set up this little adventure so he could get Branson and Geoffrey all to himself. She and Alissa would die. Their bodies, whatever the coyotes and crows didn't eat, would dry up and float away on the hot breeze. BJ would come to look for them. Branson's father would come, too. But eventually they'd give up and go back to Philadelphia.

Leah wiped her nose. *Stop stupid thoughts .Don't be morbid.*

Alissa's dark little head popped up from the earth like a gopher on a golf course. She waved a slip of paper. "Looky. This was right here, with this turquoise."

Leah read. "'Due north. Sight off Aztec Peak. One mile.' Good lord, so this is right, after all!"

"Sure it is, Mom. It's a treasure hunt!"

Within a few hundred feet, Alissa spotted dog and sneaker tracks and scooted ahead to find more. "I am the champion scout," she singsonged. "The champion scout, the champion scout."

As daylight grew dim and the air cooled, they arrived at a large, flat, stone outcrop, wide as a football field. There were no more tracks to follow. They wandered across the rock until it ended in a cliff, a sheer, forty-foot drop into yet another canyon.

Nowhere to go. *One more hour of daylight. Half a bottle of water.*

Alissa squatted beside her. Overhead, vapor trails crisscrossed, the planes bound for Philadelphia or Los Angeles. A lizard skittered over her hand.

Leah sensed a presence—the same breathless clamminess that made her avoid dark basements and caves. She turned her head to the right. Two hundred feet away, Geoffrey, Branson, Howlin' Jim and Chaco leaned against a hand-built wall.

She was overwhelmed with relief—and then, with anger. She strode across the rock toward them. Geoffrey, shirtless, his shoulders burned bright pink, jumped up and flung his arms around her waist.

"Kaibito," said Howlin' Jim.

Geoffrey plunked back onto the rock. His face was smeared, his eyes watery.

Leah grabbed Branson by the shoulders and shook him. "What the hell is wrong with you?"

He smiled and pulled her down to the rock beside him. "You found us. This is the ruin."

She pushed him away. "How do we get out of here?"

"Mom—"

"Geoffrey, are you okay? Come here."

Geoffrey started to stand up, glanced at Jim, and sat back down. "You have to call me Kaibito now, Mom. It's my new name."

"I will not call you any idiotic name. Now, come here and eat something. Alissa, bring me my backpack."

She pulled apples and energy bars out of the pack, but Geoffrey didn't move from his spot beside the silent men.

"Geoffrey, you have to eat."

"We ate, Mom. Jim showed us how to catch things."

She stared at her son's filthy face. His necklace now included feathers and a tiny, complete jawbone, with flesh still clinging to it. "What?" she demanded, poking at the thing.

"Gila monster," Geoffrey said, thrilled and repulsed. "He showed us how to take the poison out."

"Damn it, Geoffrey!" She yanked at the leather thong, trying to get it off his neck, crushing the little bones and feathers.

"Ow, Mom!"

"Get up. We're going home. You have school in the morning." She wheeled toward Jim. "Where's the goddamned trail?"

"Can't explain it. I'd have to show you."

"I'll find it myself."

"Sun's setting. It would be wise to wait until morning."

Branson reached up to take her hand. "Leah. We're in a good place. There's lots to learn if we stay here."

"Get away from me."

"Very few people know of this ruin," said Jim.

"It's a special spot," said Branson. "I want you to share it with me."

"Oh, can the crap. It's a pile of rocks in the desert."

"I mean it, Leah. It's important to me. And so are you."

Leah sat on the wall. Branson had been in on this from the start. He never intended to go back to Phoenix that afternoon.

18

Jim, satisfied he had her, stood and pointed out the low walls of the ruin, as if he were lecturing in a classroom. "When the museum excavated," he said, "they took all the artifacts out. They put them on shelves in the basement, each piece marked with ink, maps rolled up in the corner. That's how archaeologists are responsible to the past."

"They're thieves," said Branson.

Leah rubbed her arms. "The kids don't have warm jackets. It's going to be cold tonight."

Jim said, "We're sitting at the outer wall of the settlement. This group of rooms probably supported one family group, ten to fifteen people. Small communities like this were typically located along sight lines, linking them visually with others. The museum never pursued that hypothesis, but I found two more ruins related to this one."

"Hey, Jim we've heard enough archaeology. We're tired."

"The men will sleep in the kiva, that round structure over there. Leah and the child can have this room."

He's telling us where to sleep. He's the only one who can get us home.

Jim said, "There's water about a half mile down the side. Branson will bring it. Kaibito and I are going hunting." He looked at Leah. "Gather firewood." Without another word, he turned and walked out onto the desert.

Branson picked up his water bottles and strode to the canyon rim, then disappeared. Geoffrey looked at his mother—not asking, not pleading—and stood to follow Howlin' Jim into the twilight.

Chapter 4

Awake before first light, Leah felt a chill run through her like a steel cable. She took in the huge sky with its fading stars, the rock wall, her sleeping daughter. She could hear the easy breathing of Branson and Geoffrey, snoring in the kiva like good little Indians.

She'd seen museum dioramas of ancient life. She could imagine the Hohokam rooms fully built and chinked, the ancient people huddled around cozy fires. The roof beams had disintegrated centuries ago, the upper stones had fallen, and sand had blown in, almost obliterating the ancient walls.

Last night, staring into the fire, Branson and Jim could have passed for ancients themselves. When Jim finally spoke, he resumed his lecture.

"The ruin is sacred," he said. "The spirits of the people still live here."

And I'm Geronimo, Leah thought. She sat far away from them, refusing to take warmth from Jim's fire.

"Just staying alive was a daily struggle," he said. "Yet they had enough conviction to build a kiva, the physical manifestation of their spirituality."

Alissa whispered to her mother, "What's a conviction?"

"It's what Jim deserves for dragging us out here," Leah whispered, and giggled despite her anger.

She had managed to sleep most of the night, her fury and exhaustion keeping her warm enough. Now she slipped her sneakers on, crawled out the keyhole door of their dry-stack stone room, and inched along the wall toward the kiva. As she hugged herself against the cold dark air, she studied the rounded shelf of the kiva and made out two sleeping forms—not three. Geoffrey, Branson; where was Jim?

Her body sensed a presence. Before she could turn around, a muscular hand went across her mouth. Another hand grabbed her wrist.

20

"Ge'h," he growled into her ear. He slowly released his grip on her mouth, then her arm.

"Damn it, Jim!"

"No women in the kiva."

"Oh, get off it." She pulled away from him and started down the crude saguaro-spine ladder into the kiva. She didn't dare appear frightened. Her anger was her only weapon.

"This is a men's walkabout," he called after her.

"Branson. Geoffrey. Wake up." Leah shook them, then climbed back up, hoping she looked strong and defiant. Howlin' Jim had disappeared.

"Hi, Mom." Geoffrey climbed up the ladder and sat beside her on the wall.

"This is not fun, Geoffrey."

"Jim promised to get us home early."

"Yeah, well, where is Chief Big Promise?"

"Mom? Will you call me Kaibito, just for today?"

"I will not. We're leaving as soon as it's light enough to see anything."

Chaco leapt onto the wall, and Jim materialized beside them, four water bottles dangling from his fingers.

"Kaibito, let's move."

Leah had no choice but to fall in behind the men. Jim led them in the opposite direction than Leah would have taken, but she couldn't object, because he kept the men several hundred feet ahead of her and Alissa.

She vowed to ban Jim from their household and take a firmer grip on her family. They marched until the sun was high enough to cast long shadows behind the saguaro. Even Alissa was silent, her bounce dampened.

Jim halted on a low rise. "There." He pointed far across a stretch of desert, pocked with dangerous cholla and creosote bush. The windshield of their Volvo glinted in the early sun.

"Cool!" said Geoffrey.

"Later." Howlin' Jim turned back toward the ruin.

"'Bye, Chaco," said Alissa.

Nobody spoke as they scattered the ashes of their old campfire and loaded the car. Geoffrey seemed like his normal twelve-year-old self, scampering about and tossing pebbles into the canyon; but he trod lightly around his mother. Leah took the wheel of the Volvo herself and would not look at Branson.

Back in their cinder block adobe bungalow, Leah snipped the leather thong off Geoffrey's neck and threw it into the trash. Her eyes warned him not to make a peep. The kids missed a day of school.

❖ ❖ ❖ ❖ ❖

Branson waited two days before touching her. He woke her in the third dawn, pushing gently against the curve of her back. Leah was lonely, tired of being angry. They made long, slow love until the streetlights clicked off and the sprinklers spurted on.

He's back, Leah thought, luxuriating in her mound of pillows as he slept beside her. *For now.*

❖ ❖ ❖ ❖ ❖

Geoffrey Ellis Senior pushed back from his mahogany desk and stared out the wraparound window, admiring how the sodden Philadelphia sky deepened the bright blue machines in Ellis Equipment's shipping yard. No manicured lawns, no sculpted trees or fountains prettied up the view from his executive office. Landscaping was fine for Public Relations and Personnel, but the President-C.E.O. preferred an honest look at what he'd created. Rows of blue tractors, threshers, trenchers, and road-building behemoths awaited delivery. He liked to remind himself—and his vice presidents and managers, whose offices also overlooked the shipping yard—of what made their company great.

"Ellis was built from the ground up," he would say, in speeches and interviews. "We're of the earth. We don't hang out in cyberspace. We don't process worthless information. We make a real product and fill a real need."

It was a simple formula that worked. Since the sixties, when Geoffrey Ellis began satisfying America's appetite for bigger, heavier machinery, his company had never stopped expanding. It outgrew one set of offices and then another, finally moving into its handsome glass-and-steel headquarters in the industrial park that bore its name.

Geoffrey Ellis might have retired years ago, moved on like any other great businessman. But why? To whom would he leave Ellis? His wife was long dead; his daughters, a doctor and a teacher, had no aptitude for business; and his last hope, Branson, had made his intentions clear long before he moved to Arizona. So he stayed on, arranging his days to look busier than he was.

His assistant knocked discreetly. "Sir? Your daughter-in-law's on the phone."

"Ah." Geoffrey Ellis lunged for the speaker button. Sally held all calls after four-thirty, except those from any of Mister Ellis' children.

"Hey, there." Leah's voice came over the speaker.

"Hey, I've been calling you since Saturday."

"Surely you have more important things to do?" She laughed.

He liked Leah's laughter, her banter, her affectionate teasing. He liked her better than his own daughters. Leah appreciated him.

"Nothing's more important than talking to you." He felt himself smile, for the first time in days. "How're the kids?"

"Oh, they're great. School's started. Geoffrey has a basketball buddy next door. Alissa has a new bike."

"So they're adjusting."

"They're fine. They miss their grandpa."

"And I miss them."

He waited a moment for an invitation. Leah had always welcomed him into their lovely colonial home, his wedding gift to them. But she didn't pick up on the opportunity now. He strolled to the window and watched a backhoe being loaded onto a flatbed.

"What's happening in the wild west?"

"We went camping. Got acquainted with the desert."

"Branson doing his archaeology thing?"

"You know Branson."

He heard sadness in her laugh. In some ways, his son must have disappointed Leah as much as he had him. Branson wasn't exactly society material, not what a Bryn Mawr girl reasonably could have expected. But Leah always managed a happy face.

Geoffrey Ellis sank back into the leather chair, setting his elegantly shod feet on the desk. He rested his hands on his stomach, caressing his abdominal muscles under the Italian shirt, muscles as firm as a young man's. "I guess I'll never understand Branson. He just loves to play in the dirt."

"At least he's digging. That's how you got your start, isn't it?"

Geoffrey Ellis laughed. "Never thought of it that way."

"He's happy here, Geoffrey."

"And you're a saint, Leah."

"You've said that before."

She was keeping it light. Geoffrey Ellis knew she was fond of him, but she never left openings for him to probe her life with Branson. He suspected that it was more peculiar than she let on.

"How about sending the kids back for Christmas? We could take the train to New York, stay at the Plaza. I bet they'd like that."

He heard the diplomatic hesitation in her voice. "Geoffrey," she said. "That's so sweet of you."

"You and Branson could go somewhere by yourselves. A second honeymoon. Go dig up pots."

"I just don't know."

"Think about it."

He ended the call before it grew uncomfortable. He ached to see his son, his daughter-in-law, especially his grandchildren—but he'd be damned if he would beg.

Leah set the phone down. Branson was standing behind her. "Your father. He's doing fine. Sends his love."

Branson leaned against the doorframe, polishing a small bone with a piece of emery cloth, stopping from time to time to check his progress.

"I didn't know you were in the house," Leah said. "I hope you didn't want to talk to him." She turned to face him. "Of course, you could call him yourself."

"Nope, I didn't."

"Branson, he'd love it if you'd call."

He handed her the bone. "This is for you. It's a whistle."

She took the bone, trying to show proper reverence. "Will it call the spirits?"

"You'll find a use for it."

"Well, thanks, I guess."

"I'm going to the artifact dealers' show. Want to come?"

"Will Jim be there?"

"Nope."

"Promise?"

"He's on a trip."

"Have you been seeing him?"

"Do you want to go or not?"

"Well, yes. But BJ's arriving this evening."

"You'll have plenty of time."

Glad to be in Branson's world, pleased he was respecting her ban on Howlin' Jim, Leah went. In the hotel parking lot, they strolled among the pickup trucks and campers and scruffy desert rats—middlemen who purchased from pot diggers in the field and sold to dealers in the ballroom. The desert rats, unwilling to pay the admission fee, waited outside with their dogs and their large sunburned wives. They reminded Leah of Jim, except that she guessed Jim wouldn't have a wife. Nor did he seem to own any artifacts.

Inside, they strolled among booths crammed with pots, moccasins, baskets, old bottles, cradle boards, weapons, cowboy gear, and thousands of items Leah couldn't identify. Many dealers seemed to recognize Branson. Unless they spoke to him directly, he ignored them.

"Here's something for you to learn." Branson pointed to a shelf of patterned ollas and dough bowls. "Those pots there, those are historics. Meaning they were made after the arrival of the Spanish in the seventeenth century. See the sheen, the glaze?"

"Yeah."

"These others are prehistoric. Mostly from between the ninth and thirteenth centuries. Flat firing, see? No glaze."

"They're all broken and glued back together."

"Most prehistorics come from excavated burials. When the owner died, the ancients broke the pots or put a kill hole in the middle to free the spirit. Occasionally you'll see a small unbroken pot, if the people had to abandon their rooms quickly, and if it wasn't crushed when the roof beams collapsed."

"There are a lot of pieces missing."

"That's because they were dug up with backhoes."

"You're kidding."

"Nope. That's why I call the diggers criminals. Digging on public lands has been illegal since the eighties. Pots still come out, though. Money's still being made in this cheeseball hotel."

Branson admired a lovely clay jar before setting it back on the table. "Bottom line, though, this is what matters. This is our link to the ancients."

"This show's a real education."

"I hate it."

"Even though you can't stay away."

"I'll be staying away. Take a good look, because you'll be staying away, too."

"Meaning?"

"Just that we won't be doing this forever."

Leah took in the huge hall with its soundboard ceiling and fluorescent lights, strolling tourist ladies in broomstick skirts. She took in the dealers whose cowboy boots and friendly smiles masked the intensity of their mission, which was to sell enough merchandise to cover their booth rental and perhaps a month's mortgage on their homes.

"It's like some Middle Eastern bazaar, where you can buy camels and drugs and machine guns."

"More like a slave market." Branson's expression turned gloomy again.

"I'm trying to follow you, Branson. Really, I am."

He took her hand. "I'm sorry. I'm not being weird on purpose. Want to know what I really think? I think buying and selling dead people's sacred objects is wrong. I think we're a screwed-up society with no respect for the past. I think we treat everything like it's made for our entertainment. The ancients weren't separate from nature, like we are. I think we should take lessons from the ancients, instead of defiling them."

She cherished his words, the most words he'd strung together since Philadelphia. He wanted her to understand. He wanted her to be with him.

Leah watched his brow crease as he surveyed the sprawl of commerce, then smooth out when he picked up a beautiful pitcher, then crease again as he looked at the price tag. Perhaps he was heading for another bout of Silent Indian.

"Maybe we'd better leave, huh?"

At least they hadn't seen Howlin' Jim. Branson had said he was on a trip. Leah hoped it would be a long, long trip.

Chapter 5

BJ's arrival was as welcome as rain on the parched desert. From the moment Leah hugged her in the baggage claim, they were laughing like the college roommates they once were. BJ was already crazy about Phoenix.

"You can see the sun here! Do you know how long since that celestial occurrence has manifest in Philadelphia?"

"When would you see the sun anyway, if all you do is work?"

"Oh man, between the bank and Armand, I've been living under a blanket."

"So you and Armand are finished."

"Please, never speak his name again. That's my request."

"Granted. And in return, I'll have rather a lot to ask of you."

BJ shone like a burnished Nubian goddess. An African-American student from Georgia, she had arrived in the freshman dorm on scholarship from her local Rotary Club, duffels crammed with athletic clothes and ambition. At first Leah thought her too gorgeous to take seriously, but BJ's personality and drive made her a star. In the years after college, BJ and Leah stayed close.

BJ was vice-president of the bank that handled Ellis Equipment's accounts—the first woman, and the first African-American, to hold that position. She surprised everyone but Leah.

BJ had everything. Almost. The combination of her beauty and her steel core had proven lethal to serious relationships. Now, mid-thirties, she was single again.

"This time, for good," she grinned. "Henceforth I shall live in splendid isolation."

"I'll pretend I didn't hear that, so you won't have to eat your words. "

"I'm serious. I'm tired of running my show, always watching over my shoulder for the guy who's trying to run his show over mine."

"Poor you, always the queen, never the pawn."

"Right. From now on, I'm a pawn. Just tell me what to do, and I'll jump to it."

"How can you follow instructions if you're living in splendid isolation?"

"Don't get technical on me, girl," BJ laughed.

As for her own life, Leah had only hinted at its weirdness, fearing BJ might opt out. Eventually she'd have to tell her about Branson and the ancients.

"I take it the Beamer's in the shop?" said BJ, struggling with the squeaking door of the old Volvo.

"No more BMW, sorry."

Branson had sold it, another step toward jumping off the consumer carousel. Unconscionable, he said, to own two cars, a television, a house full of energy-sucking appliances.

To BJ's raised eyebrows, Leah said, "We don't need two cars. Branson doesn't go to work anymore, remember? He doesn't go anywhere, except with the desert rat."

"Who?"

"Branson's friend. Used to be an anthropologist, archaeologist, something."

"Anthropologist, archaeologist?"

"He's out of town now. End of subject."

"You're the boss."

"And don't you forget it."

Leah slowed down through their neighborhood. She wanted to break BJ in gently, give her a chance to grasp that the Philadelphia Ellises now lived in one of the phony-adobe houses lining the street like boxes in a warehouse, with their computerized sprinklers rationing scraps of green lawn. "Keep an open mind," she warned. "I've got some explaining to do."

"Yup, you do."

Leah spied Jim's big dung-colored vehicle parked in front of their house. She kept driving.

"Damn, I forgot. No booze in the house. The Anasazi didn't do alcohol, you know."

"No prob."

"So let's go get a drink."

"Like I said, you're the boss."

She drove to a strip mall. They slipped into a booth at Friday's, as the noise level escalated with the after-work crowd.

"Let the healing begin." Leah drank her first margarita without pausing for breath.

BJ watched her, a line of puzzlement forming between her delicate brows. "I had lunch with Mister Ellis yesterday."

"How's he look?"

"He looks like the king of the jungle, what else?"

Leah smiled. "Everyone's still afraid of him."

"I think he's a big pussycat."

"Me, too. But that's because he likes us."

BJ sipped her margarita while Leah finished off the pitcher. "The board approved another stock split."

"Yeah. I heard. I stay in touch with the great man by e-mail."

"Thought you got rid of your computer."

"Internet café. Just a bike ride away."

BJ took another sip. "So tell me why, with enough Ellis dividend to buy a Caribbean island, are you living like the Flintstones of Bedrock?"

Leah sighed. "Branson loves the ancients."

"He loved them in Philadelphia."

"Well, his passion has flowered."

"I gotta say, girlfriend, he doesn't sound all that off-base to me. I'm having similar thoughts. The East is getting intolerable. I'm sick of consuming; get, get, spend, spend, buy stuff, throw stuff away. Banking, what's that about? Another cog in the machine."

"Oh, BJ, blah blah blah."

"I think the star I hitched my wagon to is flickering out."

"You just need a change."

"Roger that. But you know I've always been an admirer of Branson's point of view."

Leah licked the salt off her glass. "It's not just a point of view anymore. He's more like an Indian than the Indians are."

"Yeah, and?"

"Like I said, keep your mind open." Leah's eyes were filling with tears.

"My, my, you're a cheap date. One gallon of margaritas, and your heart falls in your lap." BJ handed her an embroidered hanky. "Now, what say we check in at the Ellis hovel? You can't keep me away forever."

Howlin' Jim's car was gone. After a happy dinner with Branson and the kids, Leah stopped worrying.

The kids loved BJ. Alissa, thrilled to share her room, brought out her Barbies for a tea party. Geoffrey rehashed the latest Suns game and showed her his trading cards. Even Branson laughed and was "present"—though he excused himself after dinner for a "walk," which, of course, would be a meeting with Jim.

Leah dropped it. There was too much fun to be had during BJ's visit.

Over the next few days they rode bicycles along the dry bed of the Salt River, smuggled in a bottle of wine when Branson was out, visited museums, and drove to Casa Grande to gape at the covered Hohokam ruin. BJ researched, planned forays, and infused Leah with her new appreciation for Arizona art and culture. Leah, not seeing Jim, his dog, or his car, settled into just enjoying.

One evening she was by the front window, waiting for BJ to bring mustard and relish from the market. The Volvo pulled up under the streetlight. BJ stepped out, her shapely dark legs catching the lamp's shine; a moment later, Jim's beige beater pulled in behind her. Chaco leapt out the rear window and began snuffling around the yard. BJ walked toward Jim's car like a robot.

"Damn," Leah whispered.

"You're swearing, Mommy," Alissa said at her elbow.

"Liss, run out there and tell BJ we're waiting."

Alissa started across the yard, then turned around and ran back into the house. "They're kissing! BJ's kissing Howlin' Jim!"

"Damn it to hell."

"Is she going to marry him?"

"Alissa, tell your dad to put the burgers on. We'll eat them without mustard and relish."

Branson cooked the meat. Leah set the table and called the kids. Nobody mentioned BJ or the condiments. As they were cleaning up, BJ strolled in, swinging a grocery bag. Leah refused to look at her. BJ pulled up a chair.

"Wow," she grinned. "I could eat."

After the kids were asleep and Branson left, Leah and BJ sat on the patio, staring at the cinder-block adobe wall.

"Why were you hiding him from me?" BJ said. "You knew he'd be my type."

"BJ, get a grip. He's a loony."

"So? I like loonies."

"Damn it, BJ, of all the guys you could take up with."

"I love skinny men. And he knows an awful lot about he Anasazi and Mogollon. He used to be a professor or something, right? Didn't you say something like that?"

"You sure didn't waste your time reading his pedigree."

"Hey, it was a spontaneous thing."

"He lives in his car."

"Really."

Leah tossed her glass of water at BJ. "What you need is a cold shower."

BJ jumped up and shook herself off, laughing. "I can take my own shower, mother superior."

"What about your little vow, back at the airport? How many days of splendid isolation has it been?"

"Leah, you know me. Let's just chalk it up as another of my many character flaws. That guy is too hot to waste on some other woman."

"Listen to me, my dear friend. I'm being serious now. That man does not like women."

BJ laughed again. "Couldn't prove it by me." She turned her eyes to the star-spangled sky. "Wow," she said.

Leah kept BJ scheduled, hoping she'd be too busy to see Jim; but all the museums, galleries, and bike rides in Phoenix couldn't match Jim's freakish allure. BJ started taking "walks" after dinner, and most mornings she abandoned her futon in Alissa's pink room before anyone else was awake.

BJ always did have lousy taste in men, Leah thought; but this episode was exceptional. For all his ooga-booga talk, Jim's knowledge and self-confidence had their appeal. He had already seduced Branson; the openhearted BJ was almost too easy a conquest.

In a matter of days, BJ abandoned her chic clothes for dull, vaguely ethnic skirts and a man's gray undershirt. She laughed at Leah's crack about a "fashion emergency"; but she kept the look. When she, too, showed up sporting a leather choker with a turquoise nugget, Leah said, "You're killing me, BJ. I feel the life blood trickling out of me." BJ laughed, but kept the necklace. Leah sucked it up; their friendship had outlived BJ's crushes before.

She decided she'd better study the competition. On a Friday afternoon, leaving BJ and the kids frolicking in the artificial waves of Big Surf, she looked up an Indian art dealer she'd met at the artifacts show.

Don Crawford's store was in a strip mall, sandwiched between a beauty shop and a karate studio. He played the wild-west character, with cowboy hat, Santa Claus beard, silver bolo, and arms lined with silver bracelets. His shop displayed the requisite western postcards, cactus lamps, tom-toms, and Navajo dolls seated at miniature looms.

"Nice gear," Leah said, hoping not to sound too green.

He laughed. "This here's just my merch. Come into the back."

The dimly lit room had the aura of a sanctum. Leah spotted piles of older weavings and a wall of baskets. A shelf of pots, historic and prehistoric, gathered dust. Even her minimally trained eye could see they were good.

"These are my muses," he said, taking down a graceful olla. It had a slender neck and was painted in a sophisticated cubist design. "This one's a Tonto. I got at least one killer pot from every one of the prehistoric cultures. Lot of 'em are better than you've seen at the museem."

"What's that one worth?"

He laughed. "Enough for me to retire on. Problem is, I can't let her go. I'd be a wealthy man if I sold 'em all to some *rico* in New York or Paradise Valley. Get rid of this dump and go sip margaritas on a beach. But they won't turn me loose. That's the nature of this business, Leah Ellis. The spirits just grab ya. Here, have a seat."

Leah sat in blanket-covered chairs with wagon wheel arms. "Don, I want to ask you about Howlin' Jim."

"Seems you might know somethin' about him already. He's been around plenty with yer husband, and that nice-lookin' black gal, friend of yers."

Leah flushed. "Wasn't Howlin' Jim an archaeologist?"

"Yep, so the story goes. He had quite a future, everyone used to say. Bright guy. He was in charge of a museem dig up at the Rim before he was even thirty."

"But?"

"Well, his way of thinkin' got turned around. He started sayin' folks shouldn't dig the ruins, said you can't dig up the ancients. That's how he got his nickname, for all the preaching and blaming. Made a lot of people mad, including yours truly."

"So he quit archaeology."

"Not right away. He started spending more time on the Rim, hardly ever showed up at the museem. Wouldn't turn over his maps or bring in field samples. That's how the story goes, anyhow. Showed up one day in buckskin pants he sewed himself. Get this: he didn't shoot the deer. He ran it down like he says the Indians used to do, chased it for a day and smothered it with bee pollen."

"You've got to be kidding," Leah laughed.

"Got a better one. One night the janitor sees a light on under the door of the museem lab. He finds Jim in there, holdin' up the bloody hindquarters of a bear. He's killed it with a knife and brought it in to skin it. Without fur, it looks just like a man's bottom half. Janitor runs out screamin' and calls the cops. Next day they fire him. Jim, I mean, not the janitor."

Leah laughed, appalled. It was good to hear about the younger Howlin' Jim; it made him less sinister. She got up to leave.

"Leah Ellis," Don Crawford said, following her out. "Might you be related to the Philadelphia Ellises?"

Leah shook his paw of a hand. "Nope," she said. "People are always asking me that. Nice talking with you, Don."

❖　❖　❖　❖　❖

Leah lobbed the stories of Howlin' Jim at BJ, hoping to punch some holes in her cloud.

"You see? He's a nut."

"My, my."

"That's all you have to say? BJ, if I saw him on a sidewalk in Philadelphia, I'd pull the kids inside and lock the door."

BJ looked studiously unconcerned. "Many of the world's great geniuses were misunderstood."

"Oh, please, BJ, you're too smart to mouth that mush."

"I appreciate outside-the-box thinkers. Jim's right on about a lot of it. I mean, look around you. Look at this plastic world in the desert. We've spent the last five thousand years evolving, to arrive at this?"

"Point taken. But still, BJ."

"Still, I'm having fun. You told me to keep an open mind, and I'm doing that. Why don't you give it a try yourself?"

"You don't have to be snide."

"Sorry, love. Just trust me. I won't do anything radical, as tempted as I am."

After a couple of weeks, BJ didn't show up for dinner one night. To Alissa's questions, Branson said, "Don't worry about BJ, Liss. She knows what she's doing."

Leah ate in silence, then sent the kids to their rooms to do homework. Standing in the kitchen, she stared at Branson. "Where the hell's BJ?"

He reached for her, but she pushed him off.

"You'll see her soon," he said. "Come on, Leah, let's go to bed early." He reached for her again, and she let him. He led her to their bed and began massaging her feet and calves.

Leah, knowing this tactic but pleased at his attention, let her muscles relax under his touch. She allowed his hands to wander up her thighs, didn't protest when he pulled her beneath him to kiss her stomach. Tonight Howlin' Jim was busy with BJ. He couldn't be in two places at once. Maybe in the morning she'd kick herself around for letting down her guard; but tonight, at least, Branson was hers.

In the morning, before their eyes were open, Branson's father called. "Is my banker there? I've got a question for her. The whole place just falls apart without her."

Leah knew he didn't need to talk with BJ; Ellis had an entire division to handle banking matters. It was an excuse to check in with them, to hear their voices.

"I think BJ's out jogging."

She chatted for a few moments, lounging in her pillows, watching Branson's scowl deepen as she told her father-in-law about the kids' activities, describing their life in the blandest of terms. She could feel the night's pleasure slip out of her. She'd always tried to pad the rough edges of Branson's relationship with his father. Branson had never called him, never initiated contact. And now that they were in Arizona, well—now was worse.

Branson reached across the blanket and took the receiver from Leah. He cleared his throat.

"You'll have to find another banker. BJ's not going back to Philadelphia."

He handed the phone back to Leah.

Chapter 6

Branson was ready for her reaction. Before she could leap up, he gently grabbed her wrists and drew her to him.

"Let her be," he said. "She made an important decision."

"Let her be? Let her throw away her career?"

"It became meaningless to her. She had a vision."

"BJ doesn't have visions. What she has is a severe case of the hots. Where did she go?"

"To the Rim."

"What the hell?"

Branson threw the comforter off and sat up. He edged around the bed and disappeared into the bathroom. Leah heard him turn on the shower. She felt as though she and her people were sliding down a slippery plate, tipped by a giant. BJ had taken leave of her senses. Branson loved her, but he was not interested in the couple they had been, the history they had built.

"We're going to meet them there," Branson called.

"No way. You couldn't push me up that rim with a front loader."

"It's just a camping trip," he called. "You've been wanting to go."

That's true. What am I afraid of?

She made him wait before answering. "What about the kids?"

He turned the water off and stepped into the room, wrapped in a towel. "Ask them."

On cue, Geoffrey and Alissa peeked through the door, then leapt in and plopped beside her on the bed.

"Mom," Geoffrey said. "It's, like, the coolest of all the prehistoric places. They have sites nobody's ever seen."

"So you guys are in on this."

35

"Yeah," Alissa grinned.

It's a camping trip. I love camping trips.

She tousled Geoffrey's hair, watching Branson. "You swear BJ's up there with Jim, just having a good old time in the woods?"

"Yes."

"No funny stuff? No me-Tarzan-you-Jane?"

"He'll behave."

With any luck, she'll be sick of Jim by the time we get there. That would be BJ.

She sighed, then smiled. The kids jumped up on the bed to slap high-fives before scurrying away to pack their camping gear.

Branson smiled. "Thanks, Leah. You'll be glad."

Alissa hummed in the back seat, making songs out of the names on the exit signs off I-17: Bumble Bee, Rock Creek, Horse Thief. Her little bike bounced on top of the pile in the back, crammed between the sleeping bags and the rear window.

Leah watched the landscape change as they gained altitude, climbing out of the Valley of the Sun toward the massive edge of the Colorado Plateau. Saguaro and cholla and sand gave way to evergreens and red earth. This was a different Arizona from the one she'd come to dislike, with deep, saturated colors that gradually lifted her spirits out of the desert monochrome.

The escarpment to the north loomed gray and inconspicuous, like a snake so large and languorous it goes unnoticed.

"The Rim, the Rim, the Mogo-yawn Rim," Alissa sang.

"Doesn't look so big," Geoffrey said.

"Wait till you get up on it and look down."

"So where are the cliff dwellings?"

"The Rim's not straight. It's convoluted, like a long, really jagged line. The ruins are tucked up the side canyons. The ancients chose their sites for specific reasons, to catch the winter sun, or for defense, or for proximity to water."

"Jim said he found one all by himself."

"Yes."

"A ruin the archaeologists never dug up."

"They didn't dig it up because he didn't tell them."

"That is so cool."

And that is so self centered, Leah thought. *Would he share his find with the museum? No, he'd save it to impress a twelve-year-old kid from Philadelphia.*

"BJ always hated camping," she said.

Branson laughed. "Remember how we used to bribe her with margaritas?"

"She said if God wanted people to sleep outside, why'd he give them the brains to build houses?"

Geoffrey laughed in the back seat. "BJ of the Jungle."

"I guess she just needed better reasons," said Branson.

Better reasons: great abs, narrow butt, woo-woo talk.

"She likes him, huh?" said Alissa.

Leah didn't answer. She might never have a positive thought about Howlin' Jim, but she was committed to being a sport about him, at least for now.

The town of Camp Verde nestled unpretentiously along the gray banks of the Verde River, looking much as it had in its former life as an Army outpost. The clapboard houses and strewn yards were shaded by tough, twisted cottonwoods whose roots snaked through hundreds of feet of rock to suck moisture from the inconstant riverbed. Camp Verde's agreeable climate was due its elevation, a few thousand feet higher than Phoenix.

They stopped for a break, letting Alissa zoom up and down a quiet street on her bike and Geoffrey practice his handstand.

Leah could glimpse the soul of the town in the organic layout of irrigation ditches, in battered pickups, in the faces of Indians and Hispanics and Anglos whose families had lived there for generations. She liked its downhome aura, so unlike the glass and steel of Phoenix. It was a long way from Philadelphia, but she could imagine a life among the rocks and cottonwoods and people who'd never moved, because they were already where they wanted to be.

"Let's move here."

Branson just laughed. "Who wants a milkshake?" He pulled into a Topps on the outskirts of town.

"It's almost dinnertime, Branson. Don't fill the kids with sweets now."

"We have to hike to the campsite. They'll work it off."

He took their orders and went to the counter while the rest of them hit the bathrooms.

Leah studied Branson in the garish light of the drive-in. He looked mysterious, which added to his allure. Leah saw the girl behind the window smile at him when she handed him his order. She watched him as he took extra care with the drinks and straws and napkins; at such moments she forgot her irritation and just enjoyed his physical beauty.

"To us," he proposed. His eyes met Leah's as they clicked their paper cups.

They bounced east on the Crook Highway. Geoffrey and Alissa fell asleep before they even left Camp Verde. Leah was yawning in the afternoon light.

"How far?"

"Quite a way."

"This had better be worth it."

The road left the river bottom and climbed steadily, until they were on the far western edge of the Rim. The view wasn't as dramatic as she'd hoped. They continued across dry, rolling country, the same gray rock and sandy soil as in Phoenix, but with piñon, instead of saguaro, dotting the vista. The sun blazed orange behind them.

Entering a forest of aspen and ponderosa, they passed a fire lookout tower, an empty campground. Leah's eyes drooped, then shut, then opened again.

"Can't stay awake."

"Take a nap."

"Aren't we there?"

"Rest. You'll need it."

Between slumbers, Leah glimpsed the piney wilderness below, an impenetrable carpet of trees. The road became a rocky, narrow path just wide enough to squeeze along. She looked into the back seat, saw the kids jostling about, but not waking, as they bumped through the forest in the falling light.

They entered a small clearing surrounded by ponderosa, like tribal elders at a sing. In the center stood a bright blue Ellis backhoe.

"Hey," she muttered, struggling to get the words out. "Forest Service?" Her tongue was glued to her teeth. Her eyelids were bags of sand, her brain a lump of wet cotton.

"No."

"Not Forest Service?"

Branson was in Silent Indian mode again. Leah could barely hear him say, "Criminals."

❖ ❖ ❖ ❖ ❖

Each time she awoke she remembered the storage lot at the Ellis Equipment plant, the new road graders, tractors, trucks—a proud army, standing ready to pave and plow and carry off the earth. She saw Geoffrey Ellis standing at the front of the regiment, giving orders; at his side, Branson, younger than Alissa, beamed up at him.

She looked at Branson. "I was dreaming about you and your father."

Branson clutched the wheel and clenched his jaw, his features barely visible in the failing light.

"Well, anyway," she said.

Darkness gathered around them like an overcoat. The woods were dark and lonely, the ponderosa boughs intertwined, forming a roof against the deepening sky. The branches also trapped a rare Arizona commodity, moisture. Leah breathed in the pine scent, letting it fill her lungs.

Branson stopped the car abruptly and turned off the engine. "We'll go on foot from here."

"I hope this is one hell of a campsite." Leah nudged the kids awake.

Branson opened the back door. "Kaibito. Let's move."

Geoffrey looked confused; then, suddenly awake, he stood at attention. Branson pulled out gear and loading him up. Alissa hopped from foot to foot. Leah, determined to be a good soldier, struggled into her pack.

Branson stepped into the woods and almost disappeared. "This way."

It wasn't really a trail. They ducked low branches, squeezed between tight trunks, clambered over rocks. Down, down, and then back up, hand over hand, the cliff sometimes to their right, sometimes to the left.

"Branson," she called. But he and Geoffrey were far ahead.

Suddenly they broke out of the forest; now they had to negotiate a rock face. Leah leaned her stomach into the still-warm stone and scooted her feet sideways along a narrow ledge, thankful it was too dark to see how far down she could fall. Alissa, fearless, hummed as she inched along the precipice. After rounding the rock, they picked their way through scratchy ponderosa seedlings and found Branson and Geoffrey in a clearing.

Leah poked Branson's arm. "Thanks. We really needed to climb a cliff in the dark."

"You did great. Good show, Alissa."

"But we could have fallen. We didn't, but we could've."

"Quiet now."

"What?"

"Don't speak. We're approaching the ancients. Women wait. Kaibito, come with me."

"Give me a break, Branson."

He put his hand across her mouth, as Jim had done. He glared, finger raised for silence, before removing his hand. Then he turned and slipped across the clearing, motioning Geoffrey to follow him into the trees.

"Mom?" Alissa whispered.

Leah was outraged. "Stay here. I'll be right back."

She followed them, sliding past rocks, listening for the creaks and pops of footsteps about twenty or thirty feet ahead. She moved when they moved, stopped when they stopped.

She saw a flame. Branson, lighting a match; and then Geoffrey. She caught a whiff of burning sage, heard the tweet of the whistle, the choking quality of an animal's bark. She could make out their silhouettes against the night sky. They lighted candle stubs and squatted to wait.

Leah heard rumbling, a low, vibrating beat, coming up through the earth, like drums or chanting—faint, yet right beneath her feet, as real as the thump of her chest.

"What the hell?" she muttered, and then silenced herself, because Branson turned in her direction.

The drumming reached a crescendo, then faded. Maybe it was Howlin' Jim out there doing his thing, signaling them. Maybe some Boy Scouts were having a jubilee.

"Okay," said Branson.

They stole back to the clearing, passing right in front of Leah's hiding place. She stalked their footsteps.

"We can go now," Branson said to Alissa. "Where's your mother?"

Leah stepped into the open. "Here."

"We have permission. Let's go."

"What do you mean, permission?"

But Branson and Geoffrey were gone.

I did hear something back there. So did they. In the morning, I'll figure out what it was.

After another hour, Leah needed her flashlight to keep herself and Alissa from stumbling over fallen trees and rocks. Branson and Geoffrey seemed to see in the dark. They kept just far enough ahead that Leah couldn't call them.

"I hate hiking at night," said Alissa.

"And I hate having no control over my destiny."

"I'm hungry."

"Yeah? Well, I'm pissed."

"Mom, your language."

"And I'm lost, too.

"Don't worry. Dad knows where we are."

"I'm not worried, Liss. Don't ever think I'm worried."

They left the woods and climbed up to a broad rock bench. Leah was turned around again. She had been certain the moon was behind them; but it hung like a coin over the outcrop. Branson pulled her up the last few steps.

"You made it."

Leah's flashlight picked out the walls of the ruin, three stones high, running like a long pew around the back of the narrow ledge. She traced it for several feet, until it turned a squared corner and dived into the ground. Leah held her breath, then let it out slowly. No one but an archaeologist would guess that human beings had ever stood on this site. And no one but a madman would have found it.

"Look there." Branson pointed to another wall. "There were two tiers of buildings."

That made for quite a few rooms, Leah calculated. A sizeable settlement of ancients had perched on that slender bench on top of the cliff. The site was quite exposed, but easy to defend. The ancients had their reasons.

"Like it, Mom?" Geoffrey said. "I can't wait to see the view in the morning."

"It's Sinagua," said Branson. "Early fourteenth century, after they started building masonry rooms instead of pithouses."

"So where are BJ and Jim?"

"Let's set up camp."

"Branson, I said—"

"And I said set up camp. They'll get here."

Okay, let it go. This is supposed to be fun.

"You could be a little friendlier," she muttered.

"Sorry."

"You get weird in the woods."

"I'll work on it."

Leah built a fire ring and started an efficient blaze, large enough to drive off the night chill and boil water for cocoa. The kids knew their jobs: Alissa brought firewood and Geoffrey set up the tents.

"BJ and Jim were bringing the food. We don't have anything except some apples and gorp."

"Then we'll eat that."

They had a sober meal, staring into the fire, watching the flames blacken the popping branches. On three sides of them, giant ponderosa surrounded the settlement like tall buildings; the rim side had only the vast open sky above and the forest below. Leah approved of the site. Yet this wasn't a normal camping trip. They'd always had real food, and they'd always had singing and silliness around the fire. Even Alissa was subdued, watching bits of lighted ash disappear into the starry sky.

Geoffrey said hardly a word. Sitting next to Leah, he smelled like Branson, a man's smell, the smell of sweat and campfire.

Branson spoke suddenly. "Kaibito will be a man soon."

"Get real. He's in sixth grade."

"A person is ready in his own time."

"Well, Geoffrey's time is a long way off, Anasazi Man."

"Changes are coming, Leah. Accept them, and things will go well."

"Meaning what?"

"Just that."

"Hey, Chief, you're a bit serious for my taste." She crossed over to him and plunked herself onto his lean thighs. "Why don't you tell us one of your fart jokes?"

He laughed, but then his face closed again.

"I've got a joke," Alissa piped. "There's this man with a chicken and a poodle."

"It's time to go to sleep now," Branson said.

"Let her finish the story."

"And one day the chicken says to the man—"

"Kaibito, scatter the fire. Save the big branches. For now, share the tent with your sister."

"Hey, Branson, we don't want to sleep yet. We slept all afternoon. Why don't you just lighten up?"

He squeezed her arm and nudged her in the direction of their tent. "I said it's time to sleep."

Chapter 7

Dim morning light through the yellow tent was enough to end Leah's twitching sleep. The first thing she saw was Branson, his eyes open, watching her. She turned away.

The first thing she felt was her arm, which still smarted where he had gripped it.

The first thing she remembered was the drumbeat, pounding up through the forest floor.

She wanted to cry. This camping trip, like everything she'd done with Branson lately, was going all wrong. He was back in his Indian suit. She had accepted his passion for the ancients, even cultivated a grudging admiration; but couldn't he be with the ancients and with her at the same time?

She sat up. *Where's BJ? Where's Jim?*

In sneakers and fleece jacket, Leah unzipped the tent and stepped into the chilly morning. Her legs felt like wet logs. She crossed the campsite to peer into the children's tent. Geoffrey slept with his mouth open; Alissa curled tight, like a hedgehog.

Leah took a survey of the site. It was narrow, a dot on Arizona's geological divide. In the Tonto Basin below, no chimney smoke rose from the trees; no window glinted; no road snaked through the ponderosa. From this spot, with the huge sky above and smothering forest behind, a person could feel like the only human being. She wondered if the ancients were ever lonely.

How did we find our way here, in the dark?

The camp by day looked normal enough, not haunted by spirits. Her tent and the kids' tent slumped nearby. A bit farther away was another tent: it had to be Howlin' Jim and BJ's. She crept close and listened to two sets of lungs breathing. How had they managed to slip in during the night and set up a tent without waking her?

She followed the prehistoric wall about a hundred feet, until it butted into an outcrop. Their bench narrowed to the width of a footpath, with a sheer drop down the Rim. She inched around the outcrop and found herself standing in the mouth of a cave.

It was only about twenty feet deep, with remnants of manmade walls beneath the overhang. The ancient Sinagua, or Mogollon, or whoever they were, had used the cave's roof as extra shelter for their homes. Nobody had seen this site except Jim and Branson—and now Leah.

Back in camp, she sat on the wall and stared at the third tent. She willed BJ to come out, aching and stiff, so Leah could have the pleasure of pointing out that she'd thrown away her career for a hard body and a sleeping bag.

Jim's voice came from behind her. "It's good to be up before the sun."

"Damn it, Jim!" She wheeled around, her heart thumping as if she'd run the Indy Five Hundred on foot.

He stood, shirtless, biceps twitching. The leather thong around his neck dangled some new bones and feathers. Chaco ambled over with tail at a slow wag. His cold nose touched her hand.

"You didn't hear or see me because I didn't move. Your senses will become sharper after more time in the forest."

"You think startling the bejeezus out of me will make me want to play your Anasazi game?"

"No, I don't. And it's not a game."

"How'd you get out of the tent without me seeing you?"

"I wasn't in the tent."

"Then who was in there with BJ?"

"Juana."

"Juana. Now, why didn't I think of Juana?"

Jim's mustache moved; he shrugged. "Has Branson explained the arrangements to you?"

"Arrangements?"

He looked off toward the horizon, where the sun would soon lift around the Rim's curve. "He hasn't told you."

"No."

Jim stepped off the wall and slung two gourd canteens over his shoulder. "I'll get water. Go talk with Branson." He disappeared down the hill.

Leah would not talk to Branson, not since he'd played the caveman with her arm.

She munched the energy bar from her pocket and watched the sky lighten, still disoriented. East was exactly opposite where it should be. Where were her compass and topo maps? She knew she packed them; but she hadn't seen them when they unpacked last night.

The sides of BJ's tent swayed and bulged like a bag of snakes. A moment later a girl stumbled out, swearing. She was about fourteen, fifteen at the most, stocky and solid. Her dark hair hung in a messy braid. She wore a man's flannel shirt and black tights.

"God damn," she said, stretching her arms to the wild forest below.

"Juana?"

"Hi." Her young voice exuded confidence. "You're Leah."

"I guess I am."

"Jim told me about you."

"Is Jim a—a relative of yours?"

The girl laughed, showing several fillings. "Nope. That's funny, though."

"Funny why?"

"Because my dad would kill him on sight, is why."

"Your dad might have to wait in line. There are plenty of others who feel the same way."

"Hey." Juana stood up and stretched again. "No more dad." She punched her fist at the sky. "Up yours, Dad!"

"Does your father know where you are?"

"Nope. And the only thing I'm sorry about is, I won't see his ugly face when he figures out I'm gone."

"You ran away from home."

Juana's look was pure adolescent scorn. "From a boorgie point of view, you could say I 'ran away' from what you might call 'home.' And you'd be right." She spat over the cliff. "I gotta pee." She leapt up the wall, then the second wall, and squatted behind a yucca. "You hungry, Princess Leah?"

I can be a smart-ass, too. "Do bears shit in the woods?"

"Let's get some food going. Where's Jim?"

"He went for water."

"Well, he'd better get back here." Juana stood and pulled her tights up, popping the elastic at her waist.

Jim stepped over the wall—as always, as if he'd been waiting to be announced. "Juana, we're going to designate a latrine. Don't foul the camp from now on."

"Well, hey, how was I supposed to know where's the camp and where's the latrine? Anyway, it's about time you got your butt back here. Let's eat."

"We'll eat when I say."

"Jesus, Jim, don't get your knickers in a knot."

45

Leah smiled. Maybe Leah could learn a lesson from sassy Juana.

Compared to their sodden dinner the night before, breakfast was positively jolly. They gathered around the fire, warming themselves and waiting for the sun. When BJ staggered out of the tent and hugged Leah, Leah's anger toward her melted like an ice cube on a griddle. She still refused to look at Branson; even though he cooked a whole pound of bacon and passed around the crisp slices and talked to the kids and made an effort, she chose to stay mad.

Jim shook a tiny amount of yellow powder—sacred bee pollen?—into his palm, then stirred in a few drops of oil. With BJ holding a little mirror for him, he dabbed the color on his lean cheeks. He added some black horizontals with a charred stick. Leah thought he looked like a refugee from *Cats*.

Leah held her wisecrack. Surrounded by BJ in her suit of feathers, Jim in his war paint, and a toilet-talking teenage runaway, she felt like the only sane inmate in the asylum.

As the sun slipped above the Rim, Jim stepped into the circle.

A speech, Leah thought. *Captive audience, you could say.*

"We are welcome here," Jim intoned. "The ancients are with us this morning. This is our place now."

Well, tomorrow, the ancients can have it back.

"The Sinagua and Salado, and the Hohokam before them, lived in this place. They treated it with reverence."

Oh, please. We know how to camp. Take only pictures, leave only footprints.

"Lean times are coming. You'll need to learn the ancient ways quickly."

Right. It only took the ancients several thousand years to learn them. Why are we listening to this?

"The first thing to learn is that the good of the tribe supersedes individual desires." A flake of yellow paint dropped off his cheek.

Leah laughed out loud. "I'm sorry, but this is ridiculous. Let's just take our hike."

"The women will work while the men hunt. In time, the imperative to work and hunt will become meaningful, as we strip through layers of superficiality and return to essentials."

"Please. I mean it. Can we knock this off?"

"In the evenings we'll have discussions and lessons."

Have I disappeared? Does no one hear me? Leah looked at the others. Branson was nodding. BJ focused on Jim's pectorals. Geoffrey stared at the ground. Juana picked at her cuticles.

"What's going on? Hey, Branson. BJ, what the hell?"

BJ hugged her around the shoulders. "Big doings, girlfriend."

Jim said, "If the hunt is good, we'll have meat tonight."

Leah spun out of BJ's embrace. "What are you talking about, if the hunt is good? We brought enough food for a week."

Jim sat down beside Branson. "Control your woman."

"Leah." Branson tried to touch her.

She pulled her hand away. "I can't believe you let him do this again. The kids and I are going home. You can do whatever you damn well want. Jim, where's our car? Take us to our car."

Very slowly, as if explaining to a preschooler, Jim said, "Forget your car. It belongs to the life you've left behind."

She turned to Branson. "Tell me this isn't happening."

He reached again for her hand.

"This is nuts. You can't put us through a time machine."

"Give it a chance, Leah."

"You've been planning this fantasy all along. You didn't tell me because I'd screw it up."

"Yes. I want you with me, Leah. With us."

In all their years together, his restlessness, his simmering anger toward his father, his shutting himself out of the world—all that had finally led him here. At that moment, she couldn't stand his handsome face or his wonderful hands. She hated him.

"The ancients are dead, Branson. You let Jim suck you in again."

"They're alive."

"You bastard!"

Leah rushed him with almost enough force to knock him off the log. He caught her hands and held them, dodging the kicks she aimed at his shins, and continued to restrain her until she became aware of the awful spectacle she was putting on for her children. She collapsed, sobbing, at his feet. He sat without moving, reaching out only to stroke her hair, as if she were a captive animal.

"Mom?" Geoffrey knelt by her, looking like her normal, freckled kid in a fleece jacket. "I wanted to tell you, but I was afraid you'd say no."

Jim stepped toward them. "Kaibito."

Geoffrey squeezed his mother's hand and went to stand by Howlin' Jim.

BJ shivered in her feather-studded T-shirt. "Hey, Leah. This is our big chance. New life. We're doing something meaningful. Come on and jump off with us."

Leah shook her head. "I'm trapped in a bad dream, BJ. Wake me up."

"Chodistaas," Jim said.

BJ whispered to Leah, "That's my new name. Humor us, okay?"

"I will not."

"Chodistaas was an multi-ethnic civilization, get it? I'm our resident ethnic."

"Jeezus, BJ."

"If we don't like it, we'll go back. Deal?"

"I don't like it. Let's go back."

Juana stood up. "Are you guys gonna stand around jabbering all day, or what? Because I say let's get on with this. Jim, what's this work we're supposed to do?"

Jim put his paints into a pouch and gathered his arrows, inspecting each one before sliding it into the quiver. "Cache the food. The ancients left a place at the end of that wall." He pointed to a spot in the dirt.

"I don't see any cache."

"It's circular and about two or three feet across. You'll have to go down about four feet."

"Dig?" said BJ. "You want us to dig?"

"I thought you disapproved of digging ruins," Leah sneered.

"We have permission." Jim turned to Juana and BJ. "Bring water. As you learn your tasks, you'll find talking becomes less necessary. Have the fire ready at nightfall." He shouldered his quiver.

Branson tried again to touch her, but she pulled away. He turned and followed Jim toward the forest. Leah grabbed Geoffrey and squeezed him before he, too, walked away. She watched the spot where they disappeared, just a blur against the line of ponderosa.

Alissa ventured toward her, frowning beneath her dark bangs. "What're we doing?"

"Come here, Alissa." Leah's voice caught in her throat. She sat on the log and pulled Alissa onto her lap. "Don't worry."

"What about our hike?"

"No hike today. Sorry."

She looked out over the vast forest, feeling as though the Rim beneath her were bucking and heaving. But it wasn't a signal from the ancients; it was her knees, knocking together stupidly. What must Alissa have thought,

48

watching her attack Branson? There was no way to erase that picture from a little girl's memory. All she could do was reassure her now.

"We'll find something interesting to do, okay?"

"We could go exploring."

"Yeah. Good idea."

Now Leah understood why they'd fallen asleep in the car: Branson had doctored their milkshakes. She understood why they hiked in the dark, with all the twists and backtracking. Jim and Branson had planned it that way. They might have been walking in circles, for all she knew. She felt capable of killing Branson, certainly Jim.

BJ and Juana watched her rock Alissa on her lap.

"What do you want?" she growled.

"Waiting for you to join us." BJ gave her a hundred-watt smile. "We need you."

"Come on, Leah," said Juana. "Jim told me you were hard core. Why don't you show us?"

Leah stared at them, BJ in her feathers, Juana in her attitude—equally helpless, equally naive. Under the dangerous misconception that she had a clue, they wanted her to be the alpha female.

She let out a huge sigh—her last sob, she hoped. It was time to get organized, think clearly.

They had a couple of days' worth of food. There was no road, no car, no map. She had acquired a teenager. Her son was in the woods with the ancients. Her husband was out of his mind.

Chapter 8

The water glass on the head table vibrated as Geoffrey Ellis returned to his seat, on a dais at the head of the banquet hall. Mister Ellis gazed onto the sea of smiling employees, waiting out the applause. The enormous centerpiece—lilies, iris, tulips, all out of season—jiggled in response to the movement of two hundred chairs being pushed back for a standing ovation.

"Great speech, sir. They were enthralled."

"It's easy to enthrall people with good news, Bob."

His vice presidents remained standing, waiting their turns to shake his hand. Their only duty today was to laud Mister Ellis, their president, founder, and mentor. Every one of them, after hearing his speech at the third-quarter company luncheon, could expect a substantial raise and stock bonus. Every one was the beneficiary of his largesse. Not one had ever disappointed, or run crosswise of him, twice.

The vice president of marketing presented a gold-and-crystal model of Ellis Equipment's new road grader, which was already in production. Mister Ellis lifted the model over his head, to another fusillade of applause, and took the microphone from the vice president.

"Thank you again, my friends. Now, please enjoy your dessert and coffee, and take the rest of the day off. We'll see you back at your desks on Monday."

The banquet room cleared; Geoffrey Ellis received the last congratulations, patted the last shoulder. Eventually he was alone in his office, high above the shipping lot. He pulled off his tie, hung up his jacket, and glanced at the mirror.

He looked older. "Dignified," his stylist said. He was just vain enough to have her touch up his salt-and-pepper hair every two weeks—"more pepper, less salt," she said. But even with touch-ups, vitamins, spa treatments, and personal trainers, it was inevitable that he should start looking like a man in his seventies.

He went to the huge window and watched the yard supervisor stroll through the lot, crosschecking next week's shipment the old-fashioned way, with a pen and clipboard.

On his desk stood a bowl of crisp bulbs. Every other Monday, he removed a dozen of them from the chilling drawer in the office kitchen and planted them on a bed of clear marbles. When they were ready to burst into flower, he brought them to his desk. He liked to watch their transformation from unassuming blobs to glorious blooms. Just before they reached their peak, he sent them home with his assistant and brought in the next bowl.

He ran his hand over the pink cups, caressing the fleshy skin, running his fingers up the stiff stems; he leaned down to breathe their freshness.

"Sally, you still here?" He called over the intercom.

"Yes, sir."

"Did all the ladies got some flowers from the tables?"

"Yes, sir. I ordered special vases so they could take them home. They were a real hit."

"Good, good. Did you get some?"

"The head table's centerpiece, sir. Julio and Mark carried it out to my car." Her pleased laugh came over the speaker. "If I'd known, I'd have planned a dinner party tonight, just to show it off."

"Glad you like it, Sally. And why are you still here?"

"I was just leaving."

"Better go, before I change my mind about the afternoon off."

"Yes, sir. Have a nice weekend. And congratulations again."

He watched the security lights blink in sequence—first yellow, then blue, indicating she'd left the outer office and signaled the elevator.

He stood at his computer and punched in his password. It was a word he'd heard Branson say, years ago. He liked its singularity; no one else would ever think of it.

No e-mail from Leah. That was odd, after their little pact to stay in closer touch. Particularly odd, given the end of their last conversation, with Branson cutting in rudely.

Branson. What the hell was wrong with that kid? Okay, so he wasn't a kid; Geoffrey Ellis had never made the mistake of refusing to let his children grow up. Nor did he expect them to praise him for the easy life they'd come into; their sense of entitlement was bred into them, after all. Branson's sisters, at least, remembered where the gravy train came from, and thought of his feelings now and then. But Branson delighted in being an annoyance and a mystery. In the years when he used to work for the company, he hadn't even shown enough respect to buy himself a well-tailored suit. He went his own way—never saying it, but making clear his disdain for his father's accomplishments. Like most parents, Geoffrey Ellis often wondered where he'd gone wrong.

So Leah hadn't e-mailed. She was probably just having fun with BJ. She deserved some fun. He wasn't going to wait around for her to write.

But that was odd, what Branson said on the phone. What did he mean about BJ not coming back?

He could call his golfing buddy, the bank president; but that would be awkward. He'd wait until Monday.

He took a good workout in his gym, then showered. His bathroom had the same bird's-eye view of the shipping yard. He stood under the warm spray, watching the foreman make his rounds. That foreman loved his job as much as Geoffrey Ellis loved his. Watching him check his list made Geoffrey Ellis forget about his son.

Mister Ellis had no social engagements that weekend, no dates with any of the attractive women he escorted. He drove himself home—he'd given his driver the day off—and sat down with the financial news and a low-fat dinner left for him by his housekeeper.

A stroll through his greenhouse confirmed that, despite being raided to make the centerpieces for the banquet, his stock of flowers would soon be back up to their normal glory. The bulbs were emerging on schedule; the orchids were thriving. Perhaps next week he'd clip an orchid for Sally to pin on her dress. He checked the temperature and humidity gauges, adjusted the light level.

"Good night, ladies," he whispered to his flowers.

Profiles about him in business journals made much of his talent for horticulture. He was as successful with flowers as he was with Ellis Equipment. These, too—the articles and the flowers—Branson had scorned. No matter what praises other people shouted, all Geoffrey Ellis longed for was a non-hostile word from his son.

He caressed a fuchsia bulb. "At least you like me," he said.

After the men left, Leah, BJ, and Juana sat for a long time. Eventually, Alissa wandered off to explore, and Leah stood up, her bones stiff as kindling.

Juana pulled three garden trowels from her backpack and handed one to BJ. Leah refused to take one. She watched as they scraped at the sandy, rocky soil. After fifteen minutes they'd barely dented the surface. Juana stood up, wiping her forehead on her shirttail.

"So, Princess Leah, are you gonna help?"

"The pleasure's all yours. I'm not into futility."

"Hey, we gotta stash the food to keep the bears off. And we could use some help."

"You could use a steam shovel."

BJ sat up and dusted off her droopy skirt. A flash of doubt crossed her face. "Huh," she said.

"BJ, you let me know when you've had enough."

"Jim says—"

"Jim can take a flying leap."

"Aw, come on, Leah."

"And so can you. You've made some weird moves around men, BJ, but this one wins the gold. You finally found a lunatic who's so good in the sack that you signed on as his slave. Brilliant."

BJ glanced at Juana. "It's not like that."

"No? Then what's it like?"

"I mean we haven't, we're not—"

"You mean you and the archaeologist aren't a mating pair?"

"Not exactly."

"Well, ain't that a hoot." Leah scratched her head.

She leaned against the ruin and watched BJ try to dig. Since BJ had tossed her common sense off the carousel along with everything else, Leah would have to do the thinking for all of them. She might as well begin.

Last night they'd clambered around a face of the Rim, moving generally east away from Camp Verde. Therefore, if she headed opposite the sun, she might come upon footprints or broken branches, anything to hint at the route. They'd crossed lots of rock, though, leaving no trace. Finding a way out would be a crapshoot. But maybe she'd find Jim's car, or theirs.

Damn. She didn't have keys for either car. Well, she'd try anyway. If she came across a car, the trail might become clear.

BJ stood up and threw her trowel down. "Okay, that's it."

Leah smiled. "Well, well, my dear, maybe all your brains haven't dribbled out, after all. I was worried about you."

"Chodistaas." Juana put her hand to her hips. "Don't be a wuss. The ancients didn't even have metal tools."

"Yeah, well, that was then. And that was them."

"Guess what, though, Juana" Leah said. "If you'll remember from some school trip you surely must have taken, they also didn't dig the cache down. They built the walls up, and covered the top with logs and stones."

"Huh?"

"You're standing on the roof of the cache. Over the centuries, Mother Nature filled it with dirt. Which you are now breaking your fingernails trying to dig up."

BJ surveyed their pathetic progress. "Hey, Juana. Why don't we just build a cache? It'd be easier to haul rocks than dig this stuff."

"Chodistaas, Jim said."

"Jim's not the one digging. I'd like to see him do this."

"You two are gonna get it," Juana muttered, and went back to work.

"Oh, yeah, we're really scared," said Leah. She felt like a jerk for arguing on the kid's level, but she couldn't stop.

"No unnecessary talking. Jim said."

"You know what, Juana? Being as you ran away from your father, maybe you need a new one. But I don't. And if you think digging a hole is making you points on some Anasazi scorecard, I've been giving you too much credit." She picked up her trowel and heaved it into the woods—barely missing Alissa, who was perched on the wall.

"Mom?"

"Know what else? I don't care what you do. Dig to China, see if I care." She went over to Alissa.

Rise above this, Leah. Be bigger than this.

"Mom?"

"Yeah."

"There's a cave."

"Yeah, I saw it."

"But there's another cave. It has big flat rocks and stuff. Want me to show you?"

Leah sat on the wall and sighed. "Tell you what, Liss. I'm going to go exploring."

"Goody!"

"But you should stay here with BJ and Juana."

"I want to go exploring. I want to find my bike."

"Alissa, no."

Alissa kicked at the dirt with her sneaker. "We're lost, aren't we?"

For the second time that morning, Leah pulled her daughter to her and lied. "We are not lost. We are just camping on the Mogollon Rim."

Ignoring Juana's glare, Leah packed a lunch and started down the cliff.

Walking away from the sun might take her toward Camp Verde. But in October the sun traveled a different path—northwest, southeast, something. In any event the ponderosa were so thick the sun hardly mattered.

No path, no footprint, no broken branch. Where was that big cliff they'd squeezed around? If she could find that, she might piece something together.

She built small cairns on mossy boulders, within sight of one another, so she could find her way back. After an hour of wandering, she hadn't seen one familiar tree or rock. She felt like a bug on a two-hundred-mile wide windshield, trapped by her own limited perspective.

At three fifteen, she turned back. She'd been gone for five hours. She scattered her cairns—no point broadcasting her intentions—and picked her way back through the forest. After only a few false turns, she climbed the final pitch to their ledge.

The cache hole was six inches deep. Alissa ran to greet her. Juana glowered. "Nice walk, Princess?"

Screw you, Juana. But she answered mildly, "Very nice, thanks. How about getting some firewood?"

"How about you getting it? Or don't you do that, either?"

"If you'd rather keep digging, be my guest." She began enlarging the fire circle, rebuilding the stone sides to trap heat more effectively. She didn't comment on the cache hole.

BJ and Alissa fanned out around the ruin, picking up sticks and pulling dead branches from trees. Leah dragged in another log for seating.

"Water?" she said.

Juana shouldered the gourds and stomped down the trail. Despite her anger, Leah was touched by the girl's grit. She just didn't want to be responsible for her.

As she shook out their double sleeping bag, she caught the scent of Branson—his hair, his armpits—smells that always excited her. How many more nights would they spend squeezed into that bag together, turned away from each other, not talking, not touching?

Chapter 9

The men returned at dusk with two rabbits and several small birds. Jim glanced at the cache hole and said nothing.

Juana took the offensive. "This dirt is a bastard to dig, Jim. We worked on it all day. All except for Leah."

"Stand aside."

He squatted by the fire and skinned the rabbits, then laced the carcasses onto a sharp stick and hung them over the flame. Branson ripped the tiny breasts out of the birds and skewered them like shish kebabs. He gave the remaining parts to BJ, to make use of the bones and feathers. Jim showed her how to stretch the rabbit skins on a frame to dry. Leah watched her best friend and former bank vice-president sit in rapt attention, taking lessons from the Stone Age.

The night sky was cold and studded with stars. Everyone except Jim put on hats and gloves and squeezed around the fire. Jim managed to stay between Leah and Geoffrey, making a private word impossible.

He stirred the fire and began his lecture. "We've done well," he said, although he didn't look pleased. "We've eaten a meal we caught ourselves. We're moving away from falseness."

Leah said, "Tricking us into coming out here doesn't count as falseness, I guess."

"In our new society there's only room for survival. Staying alive will occupy all your time, and it will keep you clean."

Leah put her greasy, unwashed hand over her mouth, to block another angry wisecrack.

"Some days, you'll have memories of your past. Your families, school, possessions, comforts. Put those memories out of your mind."

Alissa, huddled next to Branson, said, "But I like school."

"The people in your past lied to you. You know who those people are."

Juana raised her fist. "Right on. My goddamn father."

BJ looked up, eyes shiny. "The banking industry. And I was part of it. I lied every day."

"Oh, come on, BJ. You had a great job. You had respect. People liked you. What kind of trip are you going off on?"

"Leah, a lot of my job was horse pucky. You know that. It was just part of doing business. So I'm trying something different now, as unlikely as it may seem to you."

Jim stepped between them, regaining control of the discussion. "Parents, teachers, authorities, they've all lied," he said.

Alissa stood up. "My mom doesn't lie. My teacher doesn't lie."

"Branson," said Jim, and Branson shushed Alissa.

"Hey." Leah stood up and thrust her face into Jim's. She saw his moustache twitch and his eyes dart away. "Alissa has as much right to speak as you do."

He sidestepped her and continued, as if she were a piece of furniture. "Branson?"

"My past," Branson said, his voice catching. "My past is gone. I renounce my father. He's a criminal. I renounce his earth-ravaging business. He's my enemy."

Alissa's face was a tragic mask. "Dad, Grandpa Geoffrey's not a criminal!"

Leah scooped Alissa up in her arms. She glared at Branson. "That was a great speech, Branson. The kids really enjoyed it." She carried Alissa across the rock bench, away from the fire. "Time for bed, Liss."

"Mom?"

"Don't listen to him, Alissa. Just close your ears."

"But Dad said—"

"Don't listen, just for now. Not until he starts talking sense again."

She spent the night with her back to Branson, squeezed into the far seam of their sleeping bag. In the morning she left the tent before he opened his eyes, rubbing the stiffness out of her legs as she stepped into her jeans. A thin coat of frost lay on the fire ring.

Picking up the gourds, she started down the narrow path through the silent woods. She heard the gurgle of water, then a raspy whistle, almost like a bird's call. She listened to three short blasts, two long tweets, a pause; then again.

Water trickled into pools through a cleft in the hillside, framed by mossy boulders. Chaco, at home in the wild, snuffed around in the pine needles. Jim was naked to the waist, squatting by the stream. He had unraveled his long braid and let his gray-streaked hair fall over his thin shoulders. His leather medicine bundle lay open on the rock. Leah could see it held dried plants, a few bones, turquoise nuggets. And little bags of stuff, tied with thread—things she probably shouldn't be seeing.

He blew his whistle again, then waited, as if for an answer. He splashed water across his back and face, combed it through his hair with his fingers. Leah shivered; it must be forty degrees down here. Didn't he feel anything?

He stepped out of his jeans and splashed his crotch, giving Leah a tiny surge of pleasure to be spying on him; after all, he seemed to know every-thing about her. He was the skinniest man she'd ever seen. No wonder he turned BJ on. BJ had once said the day she met a stick figure, she'd fall in love.

Without turning around, Jim said, "When you get magic, helpers will come to you." He stepped into his jeans and tied up his medicine bundle. "You have to accept your magic before you can use it."

His crazy eyes locked hers. His face, with its sharp bones and weathered skin, was perversely appealing. She jammed her hands into her pockets—discovering, to her shame, the two turquoise fetishes he had left for her in the desert. She wondered why she hadn't thrown them off a cliff.

To break the stare, she bent down and filled the gourds. "I don't want to hear about magic."

"You will."

She hoisted the brimming gourds and started up the hill.

"Leah," he said, addressing her by name for the first time. "You dropped your whistle."

"I don't want it."

He pressed it into her palm and closed her fingers around it. A current shot up her arm, through her heart, and out her nipples. Her mouth went dry; the skin on her arms stood in tiny bumps.

"Let me go!" She threw the whistle onto the forest floor and fled up the path, into the light of the Rim.

At breakfast, still shaken by his intimate words and the jolt of his touch, she couldn't look at Jim. At the sight of Branson, she reddened like a Siamese fighting fish. She felt both men watching her as she moved around the campsite.

Jim gave the day's orders. The women were to gather pine needles and spread them to dry for bedding. "When we get enough animal skins," he said, "we'll get rid of the sleeping bags. Gradually we'll eliminate our dependency on the artifacts of civilization."

Leah didn't argue. She had to become more canny.

"In addition," he said, "you can use the day to start cleansing away the toxins of your past. Juana, you know what I mean. You won't escape unless you burn or bury those memories."

Juana glowered. "Whatever."

"What did you say, Juana?"

"I said I'll try."

Juana looked like a rained-out garage sale, her hair hanging uncombed, the flannel shirt flapping. The sun wasn't even up, and Leah was tired of her already. Still, she wanted to cut her some slack; the girl carried a heavy load.

Jim gave Juana one last, hard look. "I'll hunt alone today. Branson will take Kaibito to cleanse."

When Jim and Branson went to gather their gear, Leah pulled Geoffrey aside for a hug. His hands were sticky, and his cheeks were smeared with soot. He had added another small bone to his necklace. The fetishes clashed comically—reassuringly—with his fleece jacket and all-American face. Leah held him to her and breathed in the scent of his hair.

"Geoffrey, is your past so terrible you have to burn it out?"

"Aw, Mom, it's just something we all do."

"Well, I don't."

"It's okay if you don't." He held her tight around her waist.

"And I will not call you Kaibito."

He grinned. "You don't have to."

"Geoffrey, I'm going to tell you something. You're not to tell anyone."

"I won't."

"I'm getting us out of here. We're not going to live with the ancients one day longer than I can help it."

"Mom—"

"Don't argue. I'm going to get my magic, and then I'm getting us out of here."

He gave her a quick squeeze and joined his father.

Once BJ and Juana had begun their pine-bough quest, Leah followed Alissa to see her discoveries. The little girl skipped along the edge of the cliff as if she'd been born there, sure-footed, happy to be adventuring. They passed the first cave, with its low ancient walls, and continued several hundred feet farther around the ledge. The second cave was twice as deep. Bats flitted about the ceiling, settling onto thick ponderosa roots that clung to the rocky walls.

In the dim light at the rear, they found knee-high slabs set in three crude circles, each ring about four feet across, like miniature Stonehenges. Leah figured the slabs to be about four feet long—huge pieces for a little Sinagua ancient to haul into place.

The sand was easy to dig, and they got down several inches using just their hands. They scattered the sand, rather than piling it, and disguised their digging with branches and leaves.

"Why are we digging these up?" Alissa asked, as they stood to examine the morning's work.

"I think there's something down there."

"Pots?"

"I don't know. But it's our secret."

Back in camp, BJ and Juana readily obeyed her order to take a break from stripping pine needles. As on the day before, their progress was not impressive; their pile of needles wouldn't make a bed for a housecat. They stretched out on the low wall, groaning and rubbing their backs.

"Pulling apart trees is not my thing," said BJ. Sap clung to her fingers and face. The feathers on her T-shirt were frazzled and sticky.

"So what is your thing?"

"I'll let you know when I figure it out, hon. Meanwhile, allow me to concentrate on the higher purpose."

Juana blew her nose on her sleeve. "I suppose you're going for your afternoon stroll, Princess Leah?"

"Yes, I am. What about that cleanse of yours, Juana?"

"I don't know how to do it. I don't want to go into the woods by myself."

"Chief's orders."

"He's not my chief."

"I'm afraid he is."

"He can't make me do it."

"Up to you."

Leah was pleased at Juana's hint of rebellion. She also found herself comfortable in her alpha-female role. She'd always been a follower; now she had three underlings. Maybe her magic was about taking the lead.

But if that was all it was, there were probably easier ways to learn it. Workshops, seminars. For credit, even.

"Whatever," she said.

On her next foray into the woods, Leah took deep breaths to calm herself, sited her course from cairn to cairn, and concentrated on the route. Three deer stood in a shaft of sunlight. They browsed on pine needles and manzanita, making clicking noises with their teeth and tongues. They worked their way closer to her, busy with their only mission, staying alive.

Animals were friends to the ancients, she thought. *Fellow citizens of the forest. Friends as well as meals.* In her former, pampered life, she used to wonder how man could kill a beautiful animal; now, she understood the capacity for killing grew with the level of hunger. She watched the deer wander away. *How long until I see them just as food on the hoof, rather than beings with souls?* That would depend on how long she went without a trip to the supermarket.

I'll make our camp the hub of a wheel. Every day I'll put in a new spoke, explore a new route. Eventually I'll find the way out.

She turned to retrace her steps. How many spokes were there in a wheel?

The sky was darkening when she arrived at the boulder with the little bonsai pine growing from a crack in the top. Just beyond it was the tree with the crooked root. She had only to climb the slope and scale the upper rocks to be "home."

A cry froze her.

When she heard it again—it sounded like pain—she dropped to her knees and moved forward.

The clearing was not much of a place, but Juana had chosen it. The girl sat cross-legged in a ray of late light, trying to be serene; but she couldn't sit still. She scratched her nose, adjusted the waistband of her tights, and settled in again with her eyes closed.

"Screw this!" she yelled. She yanked up her little shovel and stabbed at the forest floor. Eventually she managed to dig a shallow hole. She tore off her plaid shirt, pulling at the buttons so hard they ripped the fabric. She shoved it into the hole, threw handfuls and shovels full of dirt on it.

"Goodbye, Dad," she shouted. She scooped up dirt and pine needles and heaved them over it.

Still yelling, she began to comb the area, picking up anything she could get her hands around and piling it on the grave. She moved with ferocious energy, stopping only to suck on a sore finger or swear at a splinter.

Leah slithered backward on her belly. Her foot bumped something soft. She gasped, but a familiar hand grabbed her jaw, yanking her head and covering her mouth.

When she exhaled, Jim released her. She relaxed. She didn't turn to look at him. They crouched side by side and watched.

Juana finished by jabbing stubs of pine boughs in the top of the pile. They teetered like miniature trees under attack by chainsaw. The flannel shirt lay buried beneath two feet of rocks and debris.

"Stay there, God damn you." She left the clearing without looking back.

Leah turned, but Jim was gone. In her pocket was the whistle she'd dropped that morning. Her teeth clacked in the cold evening as she scrambled up the hillside. Her jacket was a thicket of pine needles, the knees of her jeans swampy.

BJ and Alissa had started a merry fire and sat before it, toasting their feet. Juana slept against the wall. As Leah scrounged through the diminishing food supply to make dinner, Branson and Geoffrey showed up with birds on a stick. Branson's clothes smelled of gasoline.

Leah wouldn't ask him about it.

Later, Jim slipped into the circle of light and added a squirrel and a rabbit to the food pile. He dressed them out, giving the skins to BJ.

"Did you do it?" he asked Branson.

"Done."

Leah watched Geoffrey. He looked away.

Jim said nothing to Leah.

Chapter 10

Over the weekend, Ellis Equipment's employees and stockholders celebrated the best quarter in their company's history. They booked tables at expensive restaurants, bought new golf clubs, paid off credit cards, made down payments on cars.

Geoffrey Ellis took no more time in the spotlight—in fact, he wasn't seen in public at all. His housekeeper left a basket of congratulations on the foyer table, where they sat unopened. Arrangements of gladioli and other pretentious flowers were signed for and handed back to the men who delivered them, to take home to their wives. Since the executives at Ellis were vacationing in London or Hilton Head, the assistant who lived in the carriage house on Mister Ellis' grounds provided statements to business reporters.

Mister Ellis granted two telephone interviews and talked to both his daughters, but he took no other calls. If Branson or Leah had phoned, his assistant would have put them through to the greenhouse.

He puttered with his bulbs, mixing a batch of a new feeding solution and recording the proportions. He built supports for a new genus of cymbidium orchid he was working on. It might be his most beautiful yet. If it were recognized by the Society, they would name it after him. Not that having an obscure parasite named "Ellisara" meant anything. After the joy of creating, accolades were redundant.

Monday at nine, he was back at headquarters, checking accounts for delivery. His employees were busy and content. His ideas and hard work provided jobs for hundreds of people and decent lifestyles for their families.

By mid afternoon he had nothing left to do. He said goodbye to Sally and drove himself into downtown Philadelphia. Parking on a quiet street lined with walnut trees, he walked the old colonial blocks. Two-story brick homes, built shoulder-to-shoulder in Benjamin Franklin's time and protected by preservation laws, still looked solid and welcoming. Now, however, they housed yuppie families instead of inner-city people in need of cheap shelter.

He stood in front of the first home he'd ever bought. In the little concrete enclosure his wife used to call the "back yard," he had set up his first greenhouse, no bigger than a closet, and started his first bulbs. His daughters remembered it, but Branson was a baby when they moved to the suburbs.

What a time that was. So full of hope and excitement, for his family, for his company. He'd made the point often, in speeches: "Without hope, without passion, you have nothing. Your accomplishments are worthless without passion."

I bet the kids got tired of hearing that sermon, he thought. But they had, indeed, followed their passions—especially Branson, much to his father's dismay.

Geoffrey Ellis sighed. *Look at me. Here I am at the top of my game, and I'm standing like a pensioner in an overcoat, watching the past.* He tipped his hat to a young mother jogging behind a stroller. The afternoon was balmy, with big leaves swirling, landing on historic stoops and catching in gutters. He walked toward Heritage Industrial Bank.

The Heritage Building rose high above the busy street, all sleek glass and steel. Its impressive marble lobby was a landmark of taste, the ground floor offices visually open, separated only by glass panels, from one side of the block to the other.

BJ's office was at street level. That was so like BJ, an expression of her sociability. And having a stylish African-American vice-president doing business in view of passers-by couldn't hurt the bank's image, either. BJ had a standing job offer from him—and several other CEOs—if she ever decided to change careers.

Today she wasn't there. Her lights were turned off; her secretary was not in evidence.

Mister Ellis strolled into the lobby, where several bank officers greeted him. A bushy-browed vice-president, followed by an assistant, rushed over to pump his hand.

"Geoffrey, congratulations. Saw you on the news."

"Thanks, Sam. How's the family? All well?"

"Great, just great. The twins are heading off for college. What brings you in today?"

"Sally said she could run the place better without me."

"Your Sally's a gem. Well, come on up. I'll get us some tea." The vice-president nodded, and his assistant scurried off. By the time the men had admired the view from the fifth floor and settled into armchairs, a gleaming tea service and a plate of imported cookies was waiting on the table.

Geoffrey Ellis poured. "I didn't see my favorite VP downstairs."

Sam Goldsmith paused a moment before adding sugar to his cup. "Ah," he said. "I was hoping you could shed some light. She's with your son and daughter-in-law, isn't she?"

"Yes. Was I imagining it, or did she give notice?"

"Sort of. May I be frank?"

"Sam, of course."

"I'm mystified. One short phone call, and that didn't come until several days past her return date. She didn't even talk to me personally. I was waiting until the end of business today."

"And then?"

"I don't know. Call you, I guess. It's the last thing I ever expected. She's been a bit overwhelmed lately, but still."

The two men sipped their tea.

"Computer?" said Geoffrey Ellis.

"Sure. Help yourself." Sam Goldsmith downed the remains of his tea and let himself out the door, waving goodbye with a two-finger salute.

Mister Ellis went to Sam's desk and typed in his password. There was still nothing from Leah. He logged off.

He sat at the desk, sipping his tea and staring out over the city; then he phoned Sally. "Any calls?"

"No, sir."

"Is the G-4 booked today?"

Sally checked the jet's schedule. "No, sir, it's free. Mister DePaul will need it for the Atlanta campaign launch, but not until Thursday."

"Tell the pilots I'll meet them in two hours."

"Certainly, sir. Mister Ellis?"

"Tell them Phoenix. They can bring their golf clubs."

The clouds above the Rim looked combed. Leah shaded her eyes as she watched planes streak overhead, their contrails crossing and dissipating along the east-west corridor.

For several days, the men had brought enough game for an evening meal—a rabbit, some birds, even a snake—but there was never extra. When the men were in camp, conversation was minimal. There wasn't much to talk about.

Leah missed Branson; she longed for him to touch her, craved for him to speak to her alone. But he made no overture.

BJ and Juana kept working, with unspectacular results. They accumulated enough pine needles to mash into soft heaps. BJ started a motley quilt by stitching the tiny rabbit pelts together with sinew. They gathered firewood, hauled water, and slept as late as they could to avoid the chill of morning.

The men slipped away before dawn, leaving Leah to start the fire. There was only half a loaf of dry bread and some instant coffee for breakfast.

Juana straggled out of the tent she shared with BJ, shivering in her black tights and short-sleeved T-shirt. Leah brought out a lightweight jacket of Branson's and wrapped it around the girl's shoulders.

"Here. Keep warm."

"I'm not cold."

"Wear it anyway."

BJ stepped out, rubbing her eyes. Her tight black hair stuck to her head in globs. Her beautiful figure was swaddled in Jim's bloody combat jacket; her eyes were dull. "Tent's too small for two people."

Juana growled. "Well, I'm, like, really sorry. Maybe I should just sleep outside." She poked at the ashes in the fire pit. "Where are the damn matches?"

"Hey, Juana, I didn't mean it that way," BJ said.

"I didn't ask to sleep with you, Chodistaas."

"I just said the tent's not made for two people."

"No shit, Sherlock."

"Hey, you two," Leah said. "What about cooperating? For the general good of our society?"

"Yeah," BJ said. "Sorry."

Juana glowered. "Okay," she said, finally.

"Look," said Leah. "I'm not qualified for the job of keeping you two out of each other's hair. And I don't want it."

"Sorry," BJ said again.

Leah worked with the women in the mornings, trying to stretch their meager food supply, ignoring her hunger, watching the others as they learned their duties. In the afternoons she ranged into the woods, walking as far as she dared. Always with hope she set out, and always with hunger and bitterness she turned her steps around.

❖   ❖   ❖   ❖   ❖

Jim licked grease off his fingers and cleared his throat to signal the start of his lecture. His eyes picked up the fire's glow. Though everyone else was bundled against the cold, he wore only a cotton shirt.

He had allowed BJ to make two braids of his hair. Then he pulled the plaits to the front and tied them together over his thin chest.

"The earliest Mogollon made pithouses on hilltops," he started. He glanced at his tribe to be sure of their attention. "Crops were undependable, and fields could be raided, so they moved into the valleys for defense. In winter, they built rooms on sunny cliff faces, like this one."

BJ squeezed closer to him.

"We're like them. We came here to escape those who steal from us. Those who steal our souls."

He looked at Leah, then Alissa, as if waiting for them to contradict him.

"Winter's coming. It's time to build shelters. We'll use the tops of the ruin walls as foundation for new walls."

Leah couldn't stay quiet. "You want us to build on top of ruins? And how does that make us any better than the diggers who tear them down?"

Jim almost smiled. "We have permission."

"Oh, right."

"The rear of the cave can be used for storage, and we'll build rooms for living in the front."

"And who is 'we?'"

"The women build the rooms."

"Of course. And what if the women don't want to build rooms?"

Jim didn't look at Leah, a sure sign that he was on the spot. *Good,* Leah thought. *Bit uncomfortable being the big chief, is it, Jim?*

He cleared his throat again. "I want you to know that this isn't personal. A division of labor is natural, and necessary for survival. The men hunt, and the women keep the camp in order."

"What if the women want to hunt?"

BJ said, "Leah, you don't want to shoot things, and you know it. Why don't you just go with the program for a while?"

Leah glowered at BJ but said nothing. *I'm hardly in a position to resist,* she reminded herself. *I can only try to be smarter than I'm being.*

Jim again had control. "If the discussion's over, I'll tell you how to build the rooms. You'll find plenty of usable stones from the Llana stratum. Their molecular structure causes them to break along right angles. Widest on the bottom, staggering break lines for strength. You've all seen examples. The child can do her share by gathering small rocks to fill the gaps. Questions?"

The next morning the women surveyed their building site. The overhang of the cave was deep enough to keep the rooms dry. The wall of the ruin, two feet high, made for a clear floor plan. Of course, they were seeing only the tops of the walls, the wind of centuries having filled the rooms with sand.

Leah admired the ancients' work. Eight hundred years before, while Europe was a hash of warring fiefdoms, the Mogollon had lived in these homes. Perhaps even lived peacefully.

BJ and Juana were almost jolly as they puffed up the hillside with their loads of rocks.

"Beats wrestling pine trees," BJ laughed.

Leah delegated most of the heavy lifting to Juana, who loved to show off her strength. Alissa scampered up and down the hill, bringing pebbles in her backpack. They made a basin by lining a hole in the sand floor with a stuff sack, and mixed mud with ground-up pine needles.

"We're inventing adobe," BJ said.

Alissa grinned. "Cool."

By noon they had raised the wall's height by three feet. They leaned against the warm rocks to gnaw on their scraps of meat. By mid afternoon they had a room of about five by eight feet, its back wall being the curved side of the cave. They left a small door and holes near the top, to hold the ceiling beams.

Standing back to admire their work, Leah realized she had forgotten her larger mission for almost a whole day. She looked with affection at BJ, Alissa, and Juana—her team—all covered in mud. Their hair and clothes were caked with drying clay.

"Bath time, ladies."

They trooped to the spring. Alissa shrieked in the frigid water, but soon she and BJ were laughing and splashing.

Leah studied BJ's slim, dark body. "You're losing weight already."

BJ laughed. "I just scrubbed off five pounds of adobe."

"You're too thin."

"You can never be too thin. She sat in a shaft of sunlight and ran her fingers through her tight, wet hair.

"I'm serious, BJ. Aren't you hungry all the time? I am."

"The ancients managed. Look, Leah, we're switching paradigms here. With change comes discomfort, you know."

"You said you'd leave if it doesn't work."

"I did, and I will. But where's the proof it's not working?"

Leah snorted.

BJ dried her hair on her shirt. "We have food and shelter and clothing. We have a society. We're moving toward the basics of existence, which is our goal and mission. We're hardly down for the count."

Branson walked into camp carrying a deer over his shoulders. Its head hung on his chest; his shirt was smeared with blood from field-dressing it in the woods. BJ gasped and looked away. Alissa stared at the animal's glassy eyes.

"Kaibito shot it," Branson said. His words were casual, but Leah heard the pride in his voice.

Geoffrey grinned. "Dad and Jim helped me."

Leah was delighted. They would feast tonight.

The women showed off the room they had built. Branson nodded approval; Geoffrey declared the chinking almost lightproof. Even Jim looked pleased as he ran his hands over the mortared rocks.

While the meat cooked, Geoffrey showed Alissa how to make a snare for small birds. They tied together the stalks of plants. Pecking at a bit of bait, the bird would trip the stalks and be caught in the contraption. Geoffrey and Alissa also invented a game of colored stones. Leah watched, silently daring Jim to criticize Geoffrey for playing with his sister; but Jim was busy hollowing out the deer hooves.

Dinner was a celebration. They had conversation, even an occasional laugh, as they squeezed together around the fire. Leah felt drunk—on food, on the day's accomplishments. She studied Branson's face as he straightened his arrows on a grooved rock. He looked so handsome, so natural, with his sprouting beard and competent hands. He caught her eyes and held them, before returning to his work.

Jim stood and began to speak. "Here is a question often posed about the ancients."

"Couldn't we skip the lecture for one night?"

His glare warned Leah not to get carried away with the revelry. "The question is, what's the minimum number required to sustain a population? How many members does a tribe need to survive?"

"Wouldn't that depend on the food supply?" said BJ.

"Most archaeologists arrive at the number thirty, to guarantee procreation. I believe that figure is too high."

"So you would put it at —?"

"As population increases, resources are taxed. Conversely, more workers mean a better division of labor."

Alissa yawned and crawled into Branson's lap. He gave her a little tickle. She giggled, then relaxed in his arms and fingered the leather strap with its bones and fetishes that dangled in the hollow of his throat.

"In nineteen-ten there were only six Yahi Indians, the last of a stone-age tribe," said Jim. "As civilization encroached on their hunting grounds, they were forced farther into the hills. When five of them died, the last man had no choice but to go to the whites for help."

"Ishi," said Leah. Branson had given her a book about this Indian. Ishi appeared one day, starving, at someone's door in California. He spent the rest of his life in a museum, a living archaeology exhibit.

"There were six Yahi," Jim said. "We are six, plus the girl. Our tribe is too small." He laid another branch on the fire.

"So what're we going to do about it?" BJ prompted. "We can't just go out and ask some more people to join us."

"Hey, it worked for me," said Juana.

Leah liked this issue coming to the surface. Maybe if the facts were laid out simply enough, they'd re-engage their brains and grasp the futility of what they were doing. She watched Jim break twigs and toss them to the flames.

"Branson and his woman are capable of bearing more children," he said. "Kaibito has shot his first deer. He's almost a man. He'll be of age for Juana soon."

Leah saw Geoffrey's eyes widen, saw Juana hide her face behind her long hair.

"You've got to be kidding."

"They should become better acquainted. They can share the small tent until Juana builds a room for them."

Juana stood up. "Just a goddamn minute, Jim."

"In a few years the child will also become useful. At that time we'll bring her a mate. For now she's the property of her mother, and will sleep with her, as Sinagua children did." Jim hooked his thumbs in the waist of his buckskin pants.

Juana began to blubber. "You asshole, Jim. Take me the hell out of here. I'll go back to high school. I'll go to reform school, I don't care."

Leah, sobered by her time in the vast woods, was beginning to understand what it meant to be a prisoner. A prisoner had no rights, except as conferred by the guard.

She watched Geoffrey, reading the clash of emotions on his freckled face. Twelve years old, and Howlin' Jim was already planning how to use his nascent manhood. None of the prisoners, sitting contentedly with full bellies, had seen this coming. And Branson said nothing.

"Well, that's that." Jim put the fire out, pushing sand over the embers. "Save the unburned wood," he instructed BJ. "Bring your sleeping bag and follow me." He headed toward the cave, toward the room the women had built.

If Leah didn't defy Jim now, she'd be his prisoner forever. She led Alissa to the tent she shared with Geoffrey and tucked her into her sleeping bag.

"It's cold, Mom," Alissa said.

"Snuggle down."

"Jim said I'm supposed to sleep with you."

"Now, Lissy, you know who you're supposed to take orders from, and it's not Jim, is it?"

Alissa giggled. "No."

"Besides, you know how loud I snore. Don't you think you're better off here?"

"Yeah." She was asleep.

When she went back to the circle, Leah saw Juana and Geoffrey sitting where she'd left them, as silent as the stones of the wall.

"Mom?" Geoffrey's voice quavered.

"Jim's your leader when you're out hunting," she said. "But I'm the boss in camp. Go sleep in the tent with your sister. Juana, you got your wish. You have BJ's tent to yourself tonight."

"But Jim said—"

"Did you hear me? I'm the boss."

"Well, okay."

Geoffrey squeezed Leah's hand. "Thanks." He slipped into the darkness.

Branson was in her tent when Leah took off her sneakers and crawled in.

Camp was silent. Not a breeze, not a murmur from the ancients interrupted the sound of her breath, and Branson's. Then she heard the unmistakable sound of sex, coming from the cave. BJ gasped, groaned. Her voice seemed to float over all corners of the Tonto Wilderness, behind every tree, like the voices of the ancients. Leah tried not to listen. She hoped the kids were asleep.

Finally BJ sighed, and all was quiet again. Jim, at least, was doing his part to increase their population.

Branson's hand was working its way under her shirt and sweater. It was dry and hard, but it stroked her shoulder blades tenderly. She pressed herself into the far corner of the sleeping bag, but he sat up and turned her over like a log in a stream.

He moved onto her. His weight was familiar, welcome; but his movements were rough and clumsy. She pushed her fists against his chest. He pulled her hands away and pinned them onto the nylon floor of the tent, holding her down, as he had never done before. He smelled of charcoal, pine needles, sweat; his bristly beard scratched her neck, and his free hand fumbled with the waistband of her jeans.

"Get off," she snarled.

But he began to move.

And she moved with him.

"Please don't leave me," he whispered. "Please."

Chapter 11

Leah lay in the tent, watching Branson's eyes flutter, listening to his gentle snore. He had cried with her last night, had whispered her name and said he was sorry for lying to her, begged her to stay with him. She had never resisted him before, no matter how crazy he got, and last night she didn't resist.

She had given in, as always. And now, buoyed by their intimacy, she dared think she had a chance against Jim and the spirits.

There was a shuffle of footsteps outside.

"Jim says everybody has to get up," Juana whispered.

"Tell Jim where he can go."

"Leah, please?"

"Buzz off."

A moment later, Chaco's nose poked against the tent, and Leah heard Jim's soft tread.

"Branson," said Jim.

Branson sat up, fully awake. "Yes."

He unzipped the tent and stepped into the cold air.

When they all stood, yawning and shivering, around the dead fire, Howlin' Jim looked at everyone except Leah and Alissa. He fixed each in turn with his eyes. Neither Juana nor Geoffrey returned his look.

"We're going on a long hunt, two or three days. We'll leave most of the venison for the women."

"Thanks a lot," said Juana. "Did I mention how sick we are of cold venison?"

"With the meat and some small game, you'll have enough to eat here. Questions?"

"What small game?" said BJ.

"Branson and Kaibito will show you the snares they've set. Check and reset them twice a day. With luck, you'll add some variety to your diet." He pulled out his little paint pots and opened them on the low wall.

"What're those for?" Alissa asked.

"In addition, I'll show you where to find standing deadwood for roof beams. While you're bringing them, observe the micro-ecology of the region. You'll see the reverse of normal vegetation. Juniper will be on top, firs below. Questions?"

"How are we supposed to cut down the dead trees?" Juana said. "With our teeth?"

"Take the hatchet. Now, Branson, Kaibito, show them the snares."

Leah watched Branson, who'd been asleep beside her only minutes before, turn and lead the others out of camp. *This is what I'm up against,* she thought. *Jim's magic is real.*

Jim caught her arm and made her sit on the wall beside him. "You disobeyed last night." He didn't release her.

She compelled herself to look at his light eyes. *You don't scare me,* she thought. *My boyfriend's back.*

"So break my arm," she said.

"I don't like to force you." He put just enough pressure on her arm to demonstrate how easy it would be to do so.

"From what I heard, it would seem you and BJ had enough going on, without worrying about where the kids were sleeping."

"I worry about the good of the tribe."

Recalling how far Juana's smart-assed remarks got her, Leah repressed her next retort. *Wisecracking is the only weapon available to the weak.* Besides, she felt his grip loosen, saw him look away. *He's a little afraid of me, isn't he? A woman in the wake of an orgasm may be a tad intimidating.*

"You can't tell Geoffrey what to do. Children belong to their mothers."

"Kaibito's almost a man."

"That's debatable."

"I don't debate." Jim let go of her arm. He mixed a smear of red powder and grease in his hand, then applied the color to his cheeks. "I'll give you time to think it over."

"I've thought it over. I'm in charge of my children. You're not." She got up and started to lay a fire. *I believe I just drew a line in the sand.*

"While we're in camp," he said. "Your son is yours."

Is this a victory? If Geoffrey was hers while in camp, it meant she could talk to him, could influence him. She would let him make up his own mind about procreating, when he was damn good and ready.

She lit the fire and poured water into the pot, staying far away from Jim. He hadn't hurt her. He'd agreed to share power.

Wow. I am impressive. Now, how do I hold on to this?

She would be aloof. She would not watch Jim paint; she would neither ask nor answer any more questions; she would not suck up. She would treat him the way he treated Alissa, as a powerless being.

She scrubbed out their cooking pots with sand, then set to splitting logs on the chopping-block stump. As she leaned down to stack the firewood, she felt his hand on her arm again. She stood, stiff and waiting.

"Do you wonder why Branson doesn't paint?"

"Hadn't thought about it."

"He hasn't earned the right. He's still in the past."

"You don't say."

"Kaibito has a chance to escape the past because he's young, but Branson may not succeed."

Leah lifted his hand off her arm and picked up another log, standing it on its end. "Nobody's tried harder than Branson."

"It may not be enough."

She raised the hatchet and brought it down on the upturned log. It didn't split. She tried again, aware of the weapon she held in her hand, its weight, its deadly edge.

"You're the leader of the women," Jim said.

"I know."

"The first time I met you, I knew you were the one I needed to pull this off."

"So you pegged me for a Mogollon, in our cheesebox in Phoenix. You've been planning this for that long."

"I've planned it for years, ever since I found the ruin. The only missing element was you. Without you, I'd never have actually gone through with it. Do you understand that you're key to our success?"

Do not be flattered. Do not buy in.

"Hadn't given it a thought. Too busy building walls and picking pine needles out of my hair."

"Our society depends on you."

She whacked the log, then set the hatchet down and tossed the two splits onto the woodpile. Jim touched her again, turning her around to make her look at him. His eyes were like the nuggets of turquoise she still carried in her pocket, hard and pastel, set above the black lines on his face.

"Don't be weak," he said. "Help me."

She turned her eyes away. "Don't you have arrows to straighten, or something?"

"I need you, Leah."

She planted the blade in the chopping block. She had to get away from him.

The women climbed a steep hillside through dense trees, sliding on a slippery blanket of pine needles, to find the deadwood. Juana stayed in the lead, not talking.

"What's with her?" BJ panted.

"She's probably pondering her future as my daughter-in-law."

BJ laughed.

"Juana's your daughter-in-law?" said Alissa. "Then she's my aunt, or what?"

"Oh, stop with your questions, Lissy," BJ said. "Nobody's anybody's anything. We're all just members of the tribe."

Leah yanked BJ's raggedy skirt. "You and Chief Howlin' Wolf gave quite a demonstration of tribal duty last night."

"You and Branson weren't so discreet yourselves."

Alissa turned. "What're you guys talking about?"

BJ grabbed her. "Look, you, we're in a race, aren't we? So why aren't you up ahead? You're gonna beat me anyway, you might as well get it over with."

"If I'm gonna beat you anyway, why do I need to hurry?"

The mesa top afforded a huge view, but it was just more forest, more unscalable cliffs. Leah was glad to be exploring a direction she hadn't tried, though it left her just as clueless as her other routes. She saw no buildings, no roads, nothing but the six points of the ancients—the four cardinal directions, plus down and up.

They found the piñon, kicked it over, hacked off the branches, and wrestled it back to camp. After a lunch of semi-cooked deer haunch, Leah sent the others to the spring.

She edged around the cliff and walked to the cave of the standing slabs. Surely, Jim had been there since Alissa showed it to her. But nothing had been moved. Her covering of brush was intact. In short order she dug through two feet of sand. Loosening one upright slab and pulling it out, she kept digging.

Her hand scraped something solid, which proved to be the rim of a pot. She dug around it and lifted it up. It was an unbroken red bowl, eight inches in diameter, plain and smooth and heavy. Its interior was matte black. It had a hairline crack in one side, which a prehistoric Indian had repaired by drilling two tiny holes and looping them together with rawhide thread.

She had seen finer pots. But this one was hers.

She turned it over. Sand, then kernels of corn, yellow, white, blue, poured out. She heaped them in a colorful pile, enough for a meal. There was something else: a glassy stone, perhaps obsidian, carved in the shape of a pregnant woman, its neck circled by tiny turquoise beads. It fit perfectly in her palm.

For the second time—the first being when Branson summoned the drums through the earth—her jaw began to chatter. The fetish seemed to heat up, to burn her hand.

The bowl and corn were gifts from the ancients; these she accepted. But the fetish, with its implication of pregnancy? *No, thanks, ancients. Are you under Jim's spell, too?* She set the stone down, then picked it up again. It was still hot.

Far back in the cave's darkness, she dug a hiding place, covered her bowl and fetish with leaves, and brushed away her footprints.

That night, the women feasted on eight-hundred-year-old corn.

BJ lounged by the fire, patting her flat stomach beneath her baggy clothes. "You're a witch, Leah. You conjured up a pot of corn."

"I did, and if you keep needling me about where I got it, you'll never get another bite."

"Okay, keep your old secret. And next time, grind it before you cook it, so we don't break our teeth."

"Next time, I'll let you cook."

"Hey, I didn't say it wasn't good."

Leah smiled. "BJ, you are a diplomat. Add that to your resume, along with peeler of bark and hauler of rocks."

"Are you starting in again? Because if you're gonna remind me about my brilliant career, I'm three steps ahead of you. And if you care to engage in a debate about the purpose of our mission, fire away."

"The purpose of our mission is to stay alive, I believe."

"No, the bigger purpose. The voluntary self-removal from an egregiously imperfect society."

"It wasn't voluntary for me."

"Leah, hon, what can I do to get you into the program? How can I convince you this is a right and good thing to do?"

"You can't."

"Then we're deadlocked."

"Looks like it. To be continued."

Juana stood up. "I'm freezing. Shit, Jim just grabbed me after school and said we're going. I didn't have time to bring any clothes."

"I'm making you a deerskin jacket," said BJ. "Soon as the goo dries off the inside."

"Great. I'm gonna look like Daniel Boone."

"Looks aren't everything. The skin kept the deer warm, didn't it?"

Alissa tiptoed across the circle of firelight and squeezed into Leah's lap. "Mom? I hear something."

"Hey, don't say that." BJ jumped up, grabbing a smoldering stick from the fire.

Yips and barks and howls pierced the thin air. They seemed to come from all sides, from inside their heads, from centuries in the past. They were joyous and mournful, a crazy chorus. BJ leapt around, looking for something to strike. Juana curled herself into a tight ball. As Leah comforted Alissa, she realized she wasn't really frightened.

The sound whirlpooled around them, as if they stood at the bottom of a huge bowl. Leah could see it. *It's a red bowl with a black interior. In the darkness of the bowl are the people, and the potential people inside of them. Outside the bowl are the howling things, the ones who steal souls.*

"It's a bowl," she said.

"What?"

But also outside the bowl, there is light and safety.

She saw the smooth, slick sides, saw herself and her tribe at the bottom. The sounds tapered, then died.

"Mom?"

"I saw something," Leah whispered.

"What? What'd you see?" BJ crouched behind her with her stick. "Was it the ancients?"

Leah smiled. "No, not the ancients. A bowl."

"A bowl? What?"

"It was a vision."

"A vision of a bowl?"

"What say we go to bed now?"

"What're you smoking? After that spook show, you want us to trundle off to our little beds?"

"Yes. It was just a coyote chorus."

BJ stayed close behind Leah. "I'm not going to that cave by myself. What if the ancients decide to try some urban renewal? What if a bear mistakes me for a piece of venison?"

"Shit, Chodistaas," Juana said. "Stop scaring us. Come on back in the tent with me."

Laughing to chase their fear, they squeezed into the tiny tent. Leah heard them nestle in; and then they were as sound asleep as Alissa in her lap.

She sat by the dying fire, listening to the forest. It seemed to stretch forever, in every direction.

It only seems like forever, she thought. *For a person whose transportation is her own feet, whose life span is barely long enough to reproduce, whose world ends at the farthest point she can walk in a day, the forest is forever. If you live in the bottom of a bowl, the bowl is your world.*

Could their hideout be in a circular canyon off the Rim, hidden under a canopy of ponderosa like a bowl under a blanket?

The Mogollon Rim was a huge geological feature, visible from space. Its rugged country had been mapped, watersheds captured by dams, campsites created, roads cut through. But had anyone since the Mogollon explored the entire area on foot?

On a topographic map, the Rim would be a series of brown lines a quarter-millimeter apart, the terrain too steep for more detailed codification. The uncharted forest above and below the Rim would be represented by many square inches of blank paper. Could their camp be set in a gigantic cavity, gnawed out of the Rim's edge?

Was it possible for streams to flow down from all directions, creating an amphitheater too large to be understood by a person on foot? Was that why, no matter how far she walked, she always seemed to be going in a different direction from the one she intended?

There's no such thing as a circular canyon. All streams flow into other streams. Somewhere, there has to be a passageway. Somewhere, their canyon had to open into the main line of the Rim.

Leah tried to link her forays on a mental map. She went up and down all the routes she'd tried, down and back, moving her imagined self the way the fingers of the ancient potter moved around the sides of her red bowl. Eventually she would find that hairline crack. If they lived long enough.

Chapter 12

Geoffrey Ellis took a suite for himself at the Desert Paradise, another for his pilots. He sent them out to the golf course, telling them to take two full days before checking in with him.

Every hour, he dialed Leah and Branson's unlisted number. No matter how he tried to wheedle the address from the telephone company, no matter how many supervisors he spoke to, he came up dry. Either the police or a court order was required to release that information, the operator said.

He studied letters from Geoffrey and Alissa, but the postmarks were from consolidated facilities that serviced huge areas. He tacked a map of Phoenix to his wall, marked out boundaries with a felt pen, and then began going over the map section by section with a lighted magnifying glass, seeking landmarks Leah might have mentioned.

At the resort's florist, he bought pots of hyacinths for himself, daffodils and tulips for the pilots, arranging to have them sent to the rooms. The clerk eyed him shyly as she wrote up the order.

"Most men don't buy themselves flowers."

"Most men don't know what's worth having."

"They're so pretty."

"And so are you, dear." Mister Ellis watched the flush creep into her neck. Not that he would dream of a liaison with her, but mild flirtations were one of the benefits allowed older men.

In the morning he interviewed private investigators. By noon he'd contracted with one whose breathtaking fee, payable in advance, assured his discretion. That evening as he watched the sun set on the Mazatzals, the phone rang.

"Score, sir," said the detective. He'd located the children's school district.

"How'd you do that so fast?" Mister Ellis was always pleased when employees performed well.

"It's public record, sir. Just a matter of research."

"Excellent. Call me when you have the school and principal."

The next morning, dressed in khaki pants and casual shirt—the daytime dress code for men in Phoenix—he waded through waves of children, searching for two familiar faces. The school was a cheerful, sunny place, with courtyards and outdoor eating areas, so different from eastern schools. He peered into classrooms. *Won't they be surprised,* he thought. *They'll be thrilled. Branson will be angry. Well, let him. I have the right to see my grandchildren.*

After scrutinizing every young face, Mister Ellis went to the office, where—after verifying his identity and dropping some bureaucratic resistance, the administrator told him the children hadn't been in school for three weeks.

"We sent an officer to the home," she said. "The neighbors haven't seen them. Any of them." She picked up a sheaf of papers. "Their file is still open."

Geoffrey Ellis was dumbfounded. "You didn't notify the police?"

She took off her glasses. "It's not a police matter, Mister Ellis. We get a lot of transient families. People will enroll their child, and then they find work somewhere else. Or perhaps there will be some difficulty with the law, or any number of scenarios. In any event, they move on."

"The parents don't come in for the kids' records when they leave?"

"Not always, I'm afraid."

"So you have no way of tracking them."

She shook her head. "You see what we're up against."

Mister Ellis leaned forward, laid his hand companionably close to hers. "Maybe you could give me their address."

"I'm afraid not. It's against the law."

"But under the circumstances?"

"I'm sorry, sir."

He considered asking her to dinner; but he could move faster on his own. "Well, thank you for your time. Perhaps we'll meet again."

She smiled. Mister Ellis was a charming man. But she had an assembly to attend.

The private investigator had no luck with the utility companies. "If they're renting, they could pay cash. Their accounts could be in the landlord's name. You can't supply any credit card information?"

"Why should I know my son's credit card?"

"Just asking."

"For all I know, he doesn't have one."

"D.M.V. hasn't issued any new driver's licenses in that name. Any medical conditions that would require specialized care?"

"Of course not. I could find out this stuff myself. What am I paying you for?"

"I understand your frustration, sir."

"Four people can't just disappear."

"Happens all the time, sir."

Geoffrey Ellis scouted the neighborhoods within walking distance of the school. He drove block after block, checking them against his map. He highlighted the ones with basketball hoops and concentrations of bikes. In the afternoon, he tailed several clutches of children who headed toward those blocks, noted which houses they entered. He then narrowed his search to ones adjacent to empty-looking houses.

A young mother wearing an apron over running shorts answered his knock.

"I don't know them," she said. "And I suggest you move on. People might be suspicious of an older man hanging about."

"I understand. I used to worry about my children when they were young, too. Thank you for mentioning it."

She softened. He didn't look dangerous. "Wait here."

A moment later she opened the door again and nudged her two children toward him. "This gentleman's looking for Geoffrey and Alissa. You know them?"

The boy said, "Geoffrey's in my class. But I thought he moved. You're his grandpa?"

"I am."

"Cool."

"Does he live nearby?"

"Mom?"

"I guess you could show him. Lead him there on your bike, and then come straight home."

Geoffrey Ellis made a little bow and thanked her. The next day, roses were delivered to her and to the school administrator.

He parked at the curb outside their bungalow. The sun was setting; children were being called inside. But at Branson and Leah's house, no lights came on, no TV; no stereo blared teen music. Mister Ellis waited in his car until the streetlights lit, then circled the block several times. After a light supper at a strip mall, he resumed his watch.

I can understand Branson moving to Phoenix. The Indians and all that. But why didn't he pick a decent neighborhood, a private school? Is he mentally ill?

Until now, Geoffrey Ellis had attributed Branson's behavior to his contrary streak and well-deserved black-sheep reputation. Perhaps there was more to it. *But Leah? Why the hell would Leah put up with this?*

He kept up the vigil until lights went out. *Okay, reputation be damned. Time to call the police.*

Leah lost track of how many days the men were gone. The venison supply was reduced to a few dry strips.

She woke to the memory of fluffing clean sheets, fresh from the dryer, onto soft beds. A rare Pennsylvania sun streamed through windows; she almost laughed with pleasure.

But the flap of sheets was just the rattle of her tent wall. Cold wind howled around the edge of the ruin, whistled as it scraped the mouth of the cave.

Alissa was a lump at the bottom of the sleeping bag. Had Geoffrey and Branson found a place to sleep, out of the wind? Did Geoffrey, with no blanket, huddle next to his father to keep warm? Did Branson hold his son, or had Howlin' Jim outlawed love?

She remembered her bowl, hidden for centuries after its creator had turned to dust. The Sinagua woman who made it must have endured days when her man didn't return, lived through winters without food. She must have longed for a warmer bed and worried about her children's safety. Yet during her short, uncertain life, she'd made objects of beauty and utility.

Leah could almost feel the woman's presence beside her in the tent. *Is your bowl my magic?* she wondered. *Are you my friend?*

The imaginary woman smiled. She had no teeth. She had already buried her mother, and soon, her daughter would bury her. Her man, if he returned from the hunt, would die of old age before he was as old as Branson.

Her heart ached for the woman who made the bowl. And it ached for her father-in-law, who was lost to them now, as lost as the bowl maker.

But there was no time to mourn. Something always needed attention: a child's stomach to fill, a fire to be coaxed, water to fetch.

Emotions would have to wait. She pulled herself out of the tent, slapping her hands on her thighs. Later, if she could get the others occupied with work, she'd give her bowl-canyon theory a practical test.

Juana swore as her slice of venison dropped into the fire. "Shit. Dumbass roasting stick."

BJ rescued the sooty food and handed it back to her. "Don't you think Alissa's a little young to be hearing that kind of language, honey?"

Alissa grinned. "I've heard her say worse than that."

"Oh, like we're in such polite society." Juana stuffed the meat into her mouth, then spit it out. "Jesus! That's friggin' hot!"

Leah sighed. "Juana—"

"Stay out of my face. You're worse than my goddamn father." Juana tried to clean her breakfast, rubbing her pocketknife across the leathery meat, then wiping the blade on her tattered black tights.

Leah used their last, precious sandwich bag to pack herself a lunch. "There's still corn left," she said. "If you add a lot of water when you heat it, the centers might get cooked."

Juana stuffed her meat in her mouth. "Why don't you take us with you?"

"I will sometime. Not today."

"When? After we've finished all the work? It's not fair."

Leah had no time for this. "Life's not fair, Juana."

Immediately, she wished she hadn't said that. If anyone knew life wasn't fair, it was Juana. The girl stalked off to the cave.

Leah slipped down the steep hillside, wearing every warm item of clothing she could find. The wind pushed against the tops of trees, making even the tallest ones bow and creak like masts of giant ships. She scurried like a bug through their enormous shadows.

Certain routes were becoming familiar. Here was Juana's father's "grave." Here was the clearing with the deer and the bonsai ponderosa. She straddled the first icy stream, studying the moss on its rocks. *North side, moss on the left, my right shoulder to the sun.* At the next stream, she positioned her body the same way. The moss grew farther to the right. At the next one, it was even father around. She appeared to be scribing a wide turn.

Yeah, she thought.

If she could continue around, eventually she'd arrive at the crack, the opening of their canyon onto the main line of the Rim.

In her little notebook she made a map of her route, using coded symbols to indicate landmarks, making the drawing indecipherable to anyone but herself. She walked as long as she dared, trying for a straight line at a single elevation. Outcrops, crevasses, and fallen trees necessitated a lot of guesswork.

This was the farthest she'd ever gone; she had to turn back. But now she had tentative confirmation of her theory, and some squiggles on paper to back it up.

The women were in a sour mood. Alissa leapt into her arms, sobbing.

"Where've you been all day?" BJ's voice was accusatory—which was not like BJ.

Juana sneered. "She's been 'out.'" She poked at the fire. "We almost finished the venison. I'm sick of venison, anyway."

"Here," said Leah, pulling handfuls of hackberries from her jacket pouch. "I found a bush before the bears got to it."

Juana pounced on the berries like a cat on a chipmunk, and stuffed them into her mouth.

"Hey, wait a minute, girl. That's dessert." BJ snatched a few berries for the rest of them.

"I don't give a shit. I'm starving."

"Did you check the snares?"

Alissa said, "I wanted to go, but they were too scared."

"Yeah, Alissa," said Juana. "Because there's bears out there. Because we could get lost. And because it's friggin' cold."

"I know the way, but they wouldn't let me go by myself."

"We don't want to lose you, honey," said BJ.

Alissa whimpered into Leah's chest. "They're just chickens. They wouldn't go with me and they wouldn't let me go by myself. Juana's a big boss-pants."

Leah, exhausted, shifted Alissa to her other knee. "Okay, you all, listen to me. Number one, I apologize for being gone all day."

Juana polished off her hackberries. "Let's just finish the damn deer, okay? I want to go to sleep."

"Two, you have to check the snares every day."

"I don't want to go out there."

"Do it anyway."

After Juana stomped off to her tent, BJ said, "If you leave me alone with that kid again, Leah, I might kill her."

"Murder may be the only cure for teenagerhood."

They laughed and stretched out by the fire. Alissa took out the pebbles she'd saved for cherrystones and started a game in the dirt.

Something had changed when Leah found her bowl and fetish; but more had to change. The others had slipped into a workaday acceptance of their situation, establishing unsatisfying routines that limited them to the least they could be. Their determination to live like ancients had confined them to a thought tunnel, impossible to think outside.

Any change to be made was up to her. But for now, she hadn't the brain power to decide anything more important than whether to add another stick to the fire or save it for morning.

"BJ, we've eaten all the deer."

BJ looked comfortable and unworried. "Yeah, I'll start tanning the hide tomorrow. I don't actually know how to do it, though."

"What I mean is, we're out of food."

"Huh."

"BJ, you have to help. You have to check the snares."

"Maybe the guys will bring back another deer."

"And maybe not."

BJ sat without talking or moving. She had always gotten by on good will and optimism. Perhaps now, Leah hoped, she was grasping the gravity of their situation.

"Yeah, okay. We'll check the traps."

"Whew. Progress."

BJ sat up. "Those hackberries were damn good." She flashed her electric smile.

Chapter 13

The officer taking the phone call listened with sympathy but little interest. Families did, indeed, drift in and out of Phoenix, as if blown by the desert wind. One indicator of the city's burgeoning population was that lists of missing persons grew, rather than shrank. Many cases were never closed.

A young investigator, reading the report, connected the words "Ellis" and "Philadelphia."

"You guys notice anything special about this?" He passed the report around the office.

"Holy Jesus, Stan. Ellis Equipment?"

"Gotta be." He plunged into his computer's database and came up with a C.V. on Geoffrey Ellis.

"You guys haven't been keeping up on your billionaires," he chuckled. "Never know when one might land in your lap."

It wasn't the first time he had dealt with rich people in stressful circumstances. Usually they sounded pitiful, as if they'd fallen off their wallets. When Mister Ellis answered his phone at the Desert Paradise, he had the voice of a vigorous young man just barely containing his own energy.

"I don't want to read about this in tomorrow's paper," he said. "What can we do to control the flow of information?"

"I understand your concern, sir."

"You didn't answer my question."

"We won't broadcast it, Mister Ellis. Of course, we do have a free press—"

"I don't need a civics lesson. Just do what you can, all right?"

"We'll handle it like any other investigation."

"Like any other discreet investigation."

"Yes, sir. I catch your drift."

"Good. Now, what about the sheriff's office? Who has jurisdiction?"

"We do, at this point, but it depends on where the case goes. We'll interview neighbors, the landlord, school officials."

"May I call you Stan?"

"Of course, sir. And you can be reached at the Paradise?"

Mister Ellis had sent the plane back to Philadelphia. "You have my contacts. Call any time. Now, I have a question."

"Shoot."

"Your wife. Think she prefers roses or orchids?"

Leah sent the others out into a windy morning, armed with sacks and a few kernels of corn. They were to gather any snared game, then re-bait and reset the traps.

"No arguing. Let Alissa lead. Stop at the spring on the way back."

The moment they left, she headed for her cave.

She'd estimated the upright slabs at about four feet long; the hole must extend two feet deeper than the level where she'd found her bowl. She scooped sand until she could haul up a slab and lay it on the ground.

Her fingertips felt something soft. Up came a piece of half-rotted fabric, on which the bowl had been sitting. It was spread over a network of twigs whose ends were planted around the sides of the hole, like an elephant trap.

Whatever was down there had lain undisturbed since the ancients left. Leah wasn't sure how to proceed, or whether she should. But it could be her magic. She pulled the sticks out, lining them up in the sand, and sat back to listen. She heard no rumble of earth, no howls. The wind at her ears seemed to carry faint voices; but she'd grown used to that.

As she dug, sand and pebbles fell a long way, returning a deep echo. She stretched out in the sand and hung over the blackness. The sound of her breathing came back to her.

She ran to her tent for her flashlight, thankful that she'd been hoarding her batteries all these weeks.

The powerful light swept an arc around the cavern. The upper walls were steep, lined with rubble. A wooden ladder, crosspieces tied with sinew, leaned against the side.

She made out the floor of the cave, at least fifteen feet below.

She saw pots. Dozens of them: bowls and seed jars and ollas lined the walls and covered the floor. Layered under centuries of dust, each one was filled with corn or beans—food for hundreds of lean days. The ancients had never cracked their nest egg.

She leaned farther into the hole, picking out its perimeters with her light. She saw an ax, propped against the wall of the cave, its stone head lashed to a wooden handle.

Then she saw the skeleton.

She recoiled like a slingshot, scooting away from the hole, panting.

When she could look again, she leaned back into the opening. The body lay on its side, knees folded to its chest, mostly held together by parchment skin that had mummified in the dry stillness. The ribcage had collapsed; a small bowl covered the skull. Nearby lay some cloth and arrows.

Leah hung upside down until her brain pounded. When she sat up, she was crying. She sobbed for the ancient, as if he had been her friend. He must have been a hunter like her son and husband. He lay there with his arrows and pots, everything he needed for eternity; and she mourned his death.

"I'm sorry I disturbed you," she whispered.

She rebuilt the cagework of sticks and laid the fabric over it. She wrestled the slabs back upright, propping them with rocks and backfilling around them until they stood firm. When all was covered with sand, she scattered branches and brushed away her footprints.

No one could tell there was a grave in the floor.

All day, Leah's discovery leapt inside her like heartburn. The ancients had sought her out, led her to them. Her link to them was as powerful as Jim's. She knew something he did not.

At dusk, hearing Geoffrey's whistle, Alissa ran down the trail to greet her father and brother. Leah smiled, watching Geoffrey lift her up for a hug, seeing Branson carry her into camp on his shoulders. Alissa talked as fast as she could, taking advantage of the fresh audience.

"You guys were supposed to be back two days ago. What'd you catch? We're hungry. Mom found some corn. I caught three birds. Wanna see?"

Despite a good hunt—several rabbits and a young pronghorn—the men were not cheerful. Chaco wobbled into camp behind Jim, collapsed by the fire, and went to sleep. Jim hardly spoke.

"Can I bring you anything?" BJ hovered around him.

"Call me when the food is cooked." He went to the cave.

Leah watched and said nothing—her new strategy. It worked for Jim, didn't it? He wanted her to learn, didn't he? She would learn, all right. She'd learn how to grab some power for herself. She watched Branson clean the game, watched Geoffrey sharpen tools, watched BJ sit back, bewildered by her lover's brush-off.

Alissa held up the bird she'd been plucking. "What's going on around here? Nobody wants to talk."

"Just tired, Liss." Branson patted her hair.

"Geoffrey, want to see my new game?"

Geoffrey glanced toward Jim's cave. "Sure."

They settled by the fire with the cherrystones, just as they used to huddle over a monopoly board in the living room. Before they'd even started to play, Jim emerged from the darkness.

"Kaibito. Don't shame yourself by playing with children. You might use your time better by visiting with Juana."

Geoffrey moved away from the fire.

"Hey, Jim, lighten up." Leah stood in front of him, to remind him of their deal. "He's in camp now."

"Ge'h."

Leah felt the power dribble out of her. "Branson? Say something."

"He's only twelve, Jim," said Branson.

"And he'll die at twelve if he doesn't grow up. He doesn't have the luxury of an extended childhood."

Branson, too, could mount only a feeble argument. "He's been hunting for days. Why not let him relax?"

"You talk like a woman."

Jim took his food away from the fire circle, eating by himself on the wall. Geoffrey ate in silence and disappeared as soon as he finished.

Later, in their tent, Leah snuggled in Branson's arms. He smelled clean after washing at the spring. His beard had grown softer. But he was so lean that his ribs poked through like the bones on a roast. He kissed her, ran his hands down her back, clutched her buttocks and pulled her to him.

Leah waited for him to speak. She longed for him to talk about the hunt—or about anything at all. She ached to share her secret.

He was asleep.

In the morning, BJ emerged late. From what Leah heard the night before, and from BJ's sly grin, she guessed Jim had rallied.

With the men in camp, she looked for ways to assert her alpha-female role. She sent Geoffrey and Alissa to make the rounds of the snares. "And bring water when you come back up," she said, with a glance toward Jim. Fetching water was woman's work.

Jim turned his back and continued straightening his arrow.

"Mom—"

"Do as I say."

Geoffrey picked up his bow. A hunter never left camp without his bow. She whispered, "Have fun. Don't hurry back."

They took off just like Jack and Jill, the gourds on ropes of sinew clacking around Alissa's thin shoulders. Geoffrey had a secret smile for Leah, thanking her for the time off. Leah smirked. *So what do you think of that, Howlin' Jim?*

Under her supervision—and with less resistance, thanks to Jim's presence—the women continued building rooms in the cave. They left slots at the tops of the walls to insert roof beams, but the logs were too thick for the holes. There was nothing to do but lay the beams across the chopping block and hack at them with a hatchet, like whittling an eight-foot toothpick.

Juana knelt over the block and jabbed at the log. "Shit," she said, as the blunt end grazed her knee, the blade just missing it. "This sucks."

Leah stood beside her. "Want me to do it?"

"No. I can."

Jim put his arrow down, took the hatchet from her, laid the beam across the block with one end propped on the low wall for support. Holding the log steady with his knee, he demonstrated how to aim the blade away from his body.

"Now you do it." He handed the hatchet to Juana.

Juana continued as before, awkward and pouting. Leah held her breath. The heavy blade seemed to land everywhere except where she aimed it, glancing off the log, sticking into the block.

"Juana. Do it as I showed you."

"Leave me alone." She grasped the handle close to the head, pulling it toward herself like a drawknife. A moment later she crumpled to the ground. "Ow! Jesus!" Blood oozed between the fingers that clasped her knee.

BJ was at her side. "Let me see, honey." She pried Juana's fingers loose. The cut was wide and deep—painful, without doubt—but no bone was showing. "Look, Juana, it's not so bad. We have to clean and bandage it, okay? Calm down, girl."

"Will it sting?"

"Yeah, some."

Juana began to sob. Leah brought the first aid kit, pulled out the peroxide and a dab of cotton.

"We'll fix you up, don't worry."

Howlin' Jim stood over them. "Let it bleed. The blood will clot soon enough."

"But it could get infected."

"Leave it."

"Jim—" said BJ.

"I said don't touch it. Do you think the ancients ran to the medicine cabinet every time they got a scrape?"

He picked up the white box, emergency supplies Leah always took when they camped. Out fell bandages, iodine, water purification tablets.

"This stuff is worthless to us. It's just artifacts of an addicted civilization." He hurled the kit over the cliff. He picked up the things on the ground and threw them, too.

Leah was in his face. "You're trying to kill us, is that it? We need that stuff, Jim. It's all we've got for emergencies."

He pushed her away—but not brusquely. "I'm sorry I haven't given you these lessons yet, because you may need them when I'm not here. I'll teach you about the body's ability to heal itself."

"Enough, already. Wounds have to be cleaned and bandaged."

"According to what you know. But the ancients had other ways. You'll see."

Juana, hugging her knee, yowled again. Jim poked at her with the toe of his moccasin, as if she were roadkill.

"Be quiet, Juana."

BJ tried to cradle the girl in her arms, although Juana was larger than she. They made an odd pieta, covered in blood, dust, and tears.

Jim stared at the women for a few moments. Suddenly he grabbed a handful of Juana's hair, hard enough to make her rise to her feet, and yanked her face toward his.

"You are a stupid girl." He stalked out of camp.

Chapter 14

Geoffrey and Alissa returned with a fat gray quail. Geoffrey was silent, like a good little Indian; Alissa was in her usual high spirits.

"Look, Mom." She held out the vial of water purification tablets. "I found it below the cliff."

Leah almost laughed. She imagined a little Sinagua ancient finding the pills, puzzling over them the way she puzzled over the things she'd found in the cavern.

Juana whimpered. Alissa hurried to her, as protective as BJ.

"Does it still hurt?"

"Yeah."

"Mom always tells me to go ahead and cry."

Juana let out a sob. "He called me stupid."

BJ rushed in. "He was just upset, Juana. Guys are like that, you know? They swear and throw things. It's how they react to stress."

"He's right. I'm a stupid dumb-ass."

"Now, you be quiet. I won't have you talk like that."

"I'm just a big fat problem for you guys."

"Quiet. We need you to get better."

Jim strode back into camp. He took a handful of leaves to the grinding rock and mashed them with a smooth stone, rendering a blackish mush. Then he added a sprinkling of powder from his medicine bundle and cut it in with the knife blade.

"Bring that," he told Leah. He lifted Juana as if she were a beach ball and carried her to his bed of pine boughs in the cave.

Under his direction, Leah enlarged the hole in Juana's tights and applied the mash to the wound.

"Look," Jim said. "These leaves are distinguishable from creosote leaves by this small fold in the stem. The powder is dried western soapberry. Soapberry has other uses, too. It can be used to stun fish. It's healing for us but poison to fish." He gave Juana a drink from his canteen.

This was another one of Jim's lessons. One minute he was remote and angry, the next, generous. He was cruel. He was kind. He was smart. He was crazy.

All evening, he tended to Juana. When BJ went to visit, he told her to bring Juana's sleeping bag to the cave.

"She'll sleep here tonight. I don't want her to bend that knee."

"Okay, sure."

"You can share the tent with the child."

"What about Geoffrey, uh, Kaibito?"

"He'll be all right."

Geoffrey had already left the campfire. Leah wondered where he'd sleep. He was accustomed to spending nights out while hunting with the men. Unfair, though, to rob him of a night of comfort in his tent.

As she'd learned to do with other outrages, Leah let it go. "Unfair" was losing ground as a consideration out here. She reminded herself to pick her battles. This one wasn't even worth complaining to Branson about.

Late into the night, she listened to Jim's whistle, droning on until it became just another sound. For a while it was a high, pleading whine. The next time she woke, she heard something like rain, and then Jim's voice, chanting. She floated on a raft of sound, waves of sleep lapping and receding, and always Jim's dialogue with the ancients.

At dawn, she could see her breath. Silence slapped her like a gust of wind. At the mouth of the cave, she smelled the skin of Geoffrey's deer, which Jim had stretched across the door of the room.

"Leah."

She no longer jumped when he materialized behind her. He stood at the side of the cave. She sidled into the cave and peeked inside the little room. Juana was asleep.

"I heard rain."

He raised his arm to show her a bracelet of tiny hooves that clicked when he moved. The sound was light, liquid.

"Were you calling the ancients?"

"Yes. For healing."

She squatted by him, leaning on the smooth rock. Moments like this, when they were alone together, usually made her queasy. Today she felt privileged.

Watch it, she thought.

His hair fell loose to his waist. He pulled it up and draped it across her shoulders. It smelled of campfire, herbs. "And I was playing for you," he said.

"Me?" She shifted away. "A serenade?"

"You know what it was."

Do not respond to him.

"Thank me by accepting my gifts and learning my lessons. There's so much I want to show you."

"I'll think about it."

"I don't make the offer casually. You know that, don't you? You remember what I told you? My magic isn't for everyone. Just for you."

The sun surged above the forest. A bright sliver of light struck their eyes.

Jim pulled back the deerskin door. "Juana. Wake up."

As Leah got the fire going, Juana wandered into the circle without limp or complaint. She let Leah soak the paste off the wound. The skin had knit, leaving only a trace of pink.

Geoffrey Ellis talked with the investigator twice a day.

"I don't want to be a pest," he said, choosing his words to sound humble. He had gone far by keeping his will of platinum hidden in a sheath of deference. People serving him tended to sympathize with him. He was just one of them, after all, only richer.

"Mister Ellis, don't worry. We appreciate your input."

"So, anything to tell me?"

"No, but I had a thought to run by you. My wife's got a thing for prehistoric pottery. Of course, they're out of our price range, but she's taken some classes, and she knows all the galleries and museums. She'd like to give you a little tour."

"Stan, what a kind offer. I'd be delighted."

After a day with the inspector's wife, Geoffrey Ellis knew more than he ever wanted to know about prehistoric Indians. She was a tireless seeker of knowledge and considered it an honor to educate such an important man.

She took him to her favorite galleries in Scottsdale and Phoenix, and asked questions leading to such detailed answers that Geoffrey Ellis felt his brain go into a slow, bored simmer.

Always a believer in compensating people for their time, he bought some pots. Trinkets, as far as he was concerned; curiosities, the kind of stuff Branson liked. He would walk out of gallery after gallery with thousands of dollars' worth of pots, until he had filled the trunk and the back seat.

To the dealers, "Jeff," as he introduced himself, was a dream client. He was impatient but polite, guarded but curious. And he paid cash. Speculation blew about like pollen.

In the evening, he set up his purchases in the living room of his suite. They were pretty, and sure, they were old. Okay. What was all the fuss about?

He was getting nowhere, and he was tired. He was bored with the Desert Paradise, the perfect weather, the immaculate golf course, Stan's wife, and the increasing friendliness of the gift-shop girl. He missed his office and his orchids.

In police interviews with Branson's neighbors, the name Howlin' Jim had come up. Children remembered the rattletrap car, the dog, the silent man with a long braid and fetish necklace.

"I think this is progress, sir," the investigator said. "A lot of the art dealers know Howlin' Jim. Your son has been seen with him."

"So? Where is he?"

"No information. No address, driver's license, not even a last name. He hasn't been seen for several weeks."

"That's significant."

"I think so."

"Why would a man be called Howlin' Jim?"

"There's probably a story there. He's a well-known figure in the business, although I gather that he's, well, anti-business. He's a puzzle, to tell the truth. Can't seem to get a profile on him. Still, he's our only lead."

Geoffrey Ellis sighed. "What should I do now?"

"I'm afraid I can't advise you on that."

"I appreciate your frankness."

"I'm sorry, sir."

Geoffrey Ellis hung up. He stared at the bowls he'd bought that day: red, black, white, all broken and glued together. Nine of them. Nice, he supposed. They'd look nice on a shelf. Put fruit in them, or something.

He checked his e-mail for the eighth time that day. The next morning he had the pots sent to the inspector's wife.

❖ ❖ ❖ ❖ ❖

The men spent another day in camp. Leah observed them: Jim and Branson hardly spoke now. Perhaps they had less to discuss. Branson was almost as competent as Jim, brought in as much game, and had a vast knowledge of the forest.

At night, when there was little to do except scrape hides, Leah began to look forward to Jim's lectures. At least they gave her something to think about, and made her less likely to blurt out something about her cave find. She sat with BJ, trying to remove bits of flesh that clung to the pronghorn skin.

Jim leaned on the log and stroked his sleeping dog's ears. "Chaco is a metaphor."

He caught each person's eyes in turn, lingering on Branson. "The male of a species is like a dog. That's why ancient societies were matrilocal."

Juana looked up from her cherrystones. "Meaning?"

"Women owned the house, the fire, the children. They could create more children. That was the source of their power."

"Bet the men helped out some on that."

"It's possible they never figured it out."

Leah and BJ laughed, but stopped short of slapping palms.

"You can't own children," chimed Alissa.

"A Sinagua site was populated by mothers, sisters, grandmothers, aunts. Men moved in and out like dogs, owning only what they carried. They had order. They worked together for the hunt, and they honored their organization, just as wolves and coyotes do."

How does he know this? Leah wondered. *Does he really talk with ancients?* She herself had felt the presence of the woman pot maker. And just knowing that a skeleton lay a few hundred feet away was privileged information, not available to the others. She couldn't dismiss Jim's lectures anymore.

"In actual fact—" Branson began.

Jim ignored him, as he ignored Alissa. "Survival of the society superseded the desires of the individual. The individual had no desires other than those of the society. The ancients wouldn't squander their emotions, any more than they would waste other resources."

"The opposite argument could be made," said Branson. "There's clear evidence at Kinishba."

"Kinishba is not evidence."

"What are you talking about?" said Leah, pleased to be witnessing an exchange of ideas.

"A child's burial," said Branson. "It includes a string of beads thirty-two feet long. Obviously, it was a treasure. It was a rare and valuable asset to the child's family and society. But they chose to bury it. Which indicates their love for the baby was stronger than their allegiance to their society."

Go, Branson, Leah thought. *Advance! Advance! Advance that theory!*

Jim didn't shift his gaze. "It only points to their investment in the future. Propitiation of the spirit forces."

"If it was just propitiation, they didn't need to wait until someone died."

"This is interesting, guys," BJ said. "Tell us more."

Jim, however, was not going to debate. "Too much listening to women."

"Women have things to say."

And you, dear BJ, are wasting your breath.

"Ancient men kept the company of men. Contact with women makes men weak. They went to women only to mate. They had kivas, for maintaining rituals and protecting themselves from debasement."

Alissa whispered to Leah, "They had basements?"

Jim gave Alissa a harsh look. "Men can't afford to be soft. No woman is allowed to turn a man away from his work."

Leah watched BJ stand and go to rub Jim's shoulders. She thought of a syllogism: *BJ is capable of turning a man away from his work; Jim is a man; ergo, Jim can be turned away.*

"Jim," BJ said softly, leaning into him and digging her thumbs into the tight muscles of his neck. "Isn't it a bit much, with the mating and the debasement and all?"

Jim glared at Branson. "A man's rank in the pack is never guaranteed. Every day he must earn the right to remain in the company of men."

In their tent, Leah snuggled next to Branson. "What was that about?"

Branson didn't answer right away. "He's concerned for the welfare of the society."

"Wake up, Branson. He won't let Geoffrey be a kid. He wants us to be in here procreating, instead of talking. How can you let him treat us like that?"

"Be quiet. He may be outside."

"He's afraid I'm trying to influence you. And I am. I want my old Branson back."

He pulled her closer and whispered, so soft she could barely hear him. "Jim says we can't sleep together every night. We're going to build a kiva."

Leah sat up. "And you have nothing to say about that?"

"He's responsible for everyone here. Every one of us is dependent on his skill and judgment."

"If he's so damned responsible, why doesn't he take us out of here so we can get a real meal?"

Branson sighed. "I'm tired, Leah." He turned away from her.

"Branson," she said. But he was asleep.

Chapter 15

The men left before Leah woke. *Come back, Branson,* she thought all day. *And bring something to eat. I'm tired. I won't make you choose.*

She was arriving at what Jim called an economy of emotion. With hunger and cold gnawing at her, and her constant search for the crack in the canyon bowl, she had no energy for the finer points of who would sleep where.

The next afternoon, Jim paced off the small room in the ruin he thought had been the ancient kiva. It was an almost perfect circle, nestled against the main ruin. The original floor would have been several feet below grade; but they would build up, rather than excavate.

Geoffrey, good soldier, began hauling rocks, piling them outside the space. Leah watched her son. His arms were becoming muscular, his freckled hands hard. He'd always been a serious boy; these days he rarely even smiled.

Branson and Jim were sitting on the wall, studying the project. Branson disagreed with Jim again.

"First, we don't have a firm date for the ruin. There is surface architecture as well as a pithouse remnant. The configuration of this room doesn't indicate a kiva."

"It will be a kiva."

Branson stood and paced off the circle. "Only eight feet. Too small."

"Not for a settlement this size."

"I say we find out with a test hole. If it's a kiva, we proceed with cobble-and-adobe and a roof entry. If it's a pithouse, we build it that style."

"You're intellectualizing, Branson. You keep going back to what you read in books. This isn't a study site. It's our home."

"But I don't think it's right."

"It may not be right, and you might be stalling."

"You think I'm stalling?"

"Stop listening to your wife."

Leah pretended not to hear.

They ended up doing it Jim's way. Every day, exhausted after the hunt, Jim still insisted the men work. Geoffrey would collapse by the fire just long enough to drink Leah's cedar-bark tea and exchange a few words before slumping off to gather stones. The wall rose by slow inches.

Watching them work, even BJ turned grim. "Why would they leave their nice warm beds to sleep in that pit?"

"Question of the hour," said Leah.

"Let 'em," said Juana.

The women were always hungry. The men's hunt, supplemented with small birds and a few dry berries, barely filled their stomachs. Leah dreaded the daily ordeal of coaxing Juana and BJ out of camp.

"You have to check the snares."

"Why don't you, Princess Leah?"

"Juana, just do it, okay?"

"You sound like Jim."

"Please, don't argue."

"Chodistaas walks too fast. I saw bear turds. We might get eaten."

Leah sighed. Juana wasn't much of an ancient, but she sure made her feel old.

Leah and Alissa gathered piñon nuts, hackberries, and walnuts. BJ managed to stitch up a stiff jacket for Juana, lining it with rabbit fur. Alissa's little sneakers, the only shoes she had brought, were full of holes. Leah wove a pair of crude overshoes from split yucca leaf. They would have been funny, if anyone felt like laughing. They were so tired and hungry that they were often in their tents before dark.

Leah, numb from the effort of surviving, worried herself to sleep. She rarely thought about Philadelphia, Phoenix, her former adoration of Branson. Nights were cold and long, days were cold and short, firewood scarce, the forest silent.

❖ ❖ ❖ ❖ ❖

Jim stepped out of the forest, blocking Leah's path. She waited, as a horse waits a command, the weight of the gourds pulling her shoulders. He put his hand to her throat—intimacy and menace in a single gesture.

"You're acquiring magic."

"Says who?"

"But you're using it the wrong way."

"You're mad."

"You're stronger than Branson, and he doesn't even know it. He doesn't understand what you're doing to him."

"What are you talking about?"

"You prevent your body from preparing to help with our survival. You reject your husband and the life you could carry."

"Leave me alone."

Howlin' Jim grabbed her arm and spun her around, encircling her with his hard body. Leah smelled his scent of grease, felt his arms holding her like the coils of a snake. He pulled her backward against his chest, slid his hand under her jacket, and pressed his palm on her abdomen. He held it there for a moment, then pulled it out and released her.

"Damn you, Jim!"

"You're not pregnant."

"You're damn right. I'm the most un-pregnant I've been in my life." She yanked her jacket down and stalked up the path.

"You resist," he called after her. "And you're strong. But your magic is weak, compared to mine."

Leah panted into camp and began cracking sticks of kindling over her knee. With shaking hands, she crouched to light them. Jim arrived moments later and sat on the log behind her. She felt his hand press the back of her knee, then begin to finger the fabric of her jeans, kneading her thigh. Again she felt the cord of electricity shoot through her. The jolt was followed by a wave of guilt.

"In the end," said Jim, "you'll come to accept."

❖ ❖ ❖ ❖ ❖

BJ's collection of pelts was growing. She had scraped them clean, then softened them over rocks with deer entrails and her own urine. Others, she stockpiled like hardtack in Jim's room, with the fur still on, to stitch together for blankets or clothing. BJ preferred sewing to cooking—which suited Leah, because she herself had no patience with sinew or bone needles.

Juana and Alissa played cherrystones by the fire. Juana had collected a set of stones, selecting them for uniformity of size and color, and she polished them constantly by rubbing them together in a little leather sack.

Jim lounged while their dinner crackled on the spit. "You're getting more skilled," he said, examining a squirrel mitten BJ was sewing for Alissa.

"Yeah. I'm going to put a cuff on them."

"Don't waste materials."

"It's just a little strip of rabbit fuzz, Jim. It'll look cute and keep her wrists warm. It's not a big deal."

Leah noted that Jim didn't respond. At least he played by his own rules—sometimes. Women owned the camp. He deferred to her and BJ, even if he ignored Alissa and criticized Juana.

Juana seemed to be as much a problem for him as she was for Leah. It was clear she was their team's third-string player; neither Leah nor Jim had found a use for her. Leah's irritation was tempered by sympathy, because she understood how the girl craved Jim's approval and knew she'd never get it.

Jim stirred the fire and added a small log. "Kaibito will need a hat soon."

BJ glanced at Geoffrey, mentally sizing his head. "Okay. I'll put on some ear flaps."

"Juana should make it for him."

Juana looked up from her cherrystones. "Fat chance. I don't know shit about sewing."

"You can learn."

"The same day I grow balls."

Howlin' Jim was on his feet, yanking Juana up by her dark braid.

"It's time you learned respect."

"Jesus, Jim, let go!"

Leah leaped between them. "Stop!"

He gave the hair a tug, snapping Juana's neck sharply; then dropped it. "Juana." His voice was reasonable. "Kaibito is going to be your provider. Don't forget that he'll be the one to keep you alive."

Juana mumbled something into the neck of her jacket.

He scooped up her cherrystones. "What did you say?"

"I said you're what I want to forget."

"You'd better grow up. You're not a child anymore." He tossed the stones into the woods. "What do you say now?"

"I say screw you."

Howlin' Jim looked at each member in his tribe. He paused at Leah's face, as if asking for help. Leah had no idea what to do, so she did nothing. Finally Jim sat on the wall, meeting no one's eyes.

"Juana says she's not hungry. We'll eat without her tonight."

She flipped her finger at him and stalked to her tent.

Leah kept quiet. Juana would just have to learn to live with Jim, like everyone else. But she took some of her quail meat to Juana after Jim went to the cave.

A few days later, Juana asked BJ to help her start sewing.

"Sure, hon," BJ said. "The tailoring department can use some assistance."

"We'll be the fashion designers to the ancients."

"Here, try this. It lies flatter if you overlap the seams instead of putting them side to side. More waterproof, too."

"I can't even thread the damn needle."

"Takes practice."

Juana laid the two pelts across her knee and began stitching them with the bone needle. "Ow, shit. I poked myself."

"Try putting it over a rock instead of your knee."

Juana managed to attach the two skins. She made a mess of it, but Leah held it up and praised her effort.

"So, you going to try that hat?"

"No way."

"What're you going to make, then?"

"Well…" Juana's olive skin flushed. "Jim's still walking around in just his shirt. I know he's cold sometimes, but he's being strong, you know, for the rest of us. So I was gonna make him, like, a fur vest."

This is what I'm dealing with, Leah thought.

Howlin' Jim stood on the low wall while Leah poked at the soles of her sneakers with a twig, trying to remove some of the mud from the tread. "Follow me. I'm going to teach you to fish."

Leah looked at Branson and Geoffrey, who were toiling on the kiva. Branson would lift a rock into place, turn it to find the best fit, remove it while Geoffrey slathered adobe, and once again set it into the wall. They didn't look happy.

"Why don't we all go learn to fish?" said Leah, not wanting to be alone with him.

"You can teach the others."

"I'll take Juana. She needs to get out of camp more."

"No."

"I said I'm taking her. Come on, Juana." She picked up the water jugs; women never returned to camp without water or firewood.

Jim started down the path, Chaco at his heel. He led them to a pool above their bathing spot and crawled beneath the overhanging cottonwood brush. Leah and Juana, squatting on the opposite side, listened to the water as it trickled into and out of the pool, just inches deep and clearer than air.

Jim's hands came out of the brush, holding some berries and a flat stone Leah had seen him use before. "Soapberry," he said. He crushed them on the stone and ground them into a fine powder, then sprinkled the dust on the surface of the water. He leaned out just far enough to add a few pebbles to the lower lip of the puddle, to slow the water's exit, then sank back under the branches.

Clearly, there were no fish in the pool. Juana yawned and flopped out on the leafy ground. "Wake me when you catch a trout," she said. "I'll eat it raw."

"Go upstream and wait."

"No way."

"Juana, I said go. Why do you argue with everything?"

"Screw you."

Jim came out of his hiding place and leapt across the stream. He yanked Juana upright by the hand.

She screeched. "Okay, I'll be quiet, Jim, I promise. I'll be respectful."

He pushed her away. "The time to be respectful is before you blow it. What does it take to teach you?"

Leah stood. "Maybe she could just go back to camp."

"I've had enough of her impudence and cowardice. She's going to learn not to be afraid of the forest. You wait here. Chaco, stay."

"Why don't you let me handle it, Jim?"

He pushed Juana's shoulders, making her stumble uphill. "Move." They disappeared into the brush.

Damn it. Why did I let him do that? Leah listened to the drip of the brook, the pop of twigs overhead. A leaf dropped to the surface of the pool and turned slowly.

I'm going back to camp. I'll show him he can't bully us. The women have to stick together, even Juana. She started up the path.

He was back, squatting on the other side of the pool. "Take out your whistle."

She fished the little bone out of her pocket, cursing her obedience. "Where's Juana?"

"Blow."

She put the whistle to her lips and produced a breathy sound, like the whisper of the breeze through the ponderosa. "This is ridiculous," she said. "What did you do with Juana?"

"Just keep playing."

She blew on the bone a few more times, eventually giving in to a lightheaded self-hypnosis. She felt as if her eyes were popping.

"I can't do this anymore."

"Ge'h." Jim pointed to the pool with a skinny index finger. Leah saw a flash of silver in the rivulet above, heard a tiny splash, then the slap-slap-slap of a thrashing tail. The trout's head poked up, the O of its mouth sucking air. Moments later, the fish floated up and hung suspended at the surface of the crystal water.

Jim scooped up the fish and held it for Leah to examine. It was solid dead.

"You called it down to the pool. That was the magic. Killing it was just mechanical."

"I have to admit, I'm impressed."

"You're learning what you're capable of." He lay the fish on a rock, gutted it, tossed the guts to Chaco, and started up the narrow path.

"Where's Juana?"

"She's facing her fear."

"I'm going to get her."

"Leave her, Leah." He stopped. "I made a mistake in thinking she could make it here. Come cook the fish." He turned and disappeared up the path.

Dusk had fallen. Under the ponderosa roof, all she could see was the glint of water at her feet. *That bastard,* she thought. *He's left her out there by herself.*

"Juana?" She started uphill. The sky was dark as a witch's cloak. She stumbled over rocks and logs, scraped her cheek on a branch, smelling the damp earth above the spring. Poor Juana was probably wandering around in circles. She climbed on top of a boulder to listen.

Juana's whimper, high and pathetic, came out of the shadows.

"Where are you?" Leah crawled down to follow the sound, but the girl, maddening as always, didn't answer. Leah moved like a blind woman, dodging sticks that poked like swords, stopping to listen.

She heard the rustle of pine needles. Inching toward a huge ponderosa, she felt the girl's shoulder.

"Why the hell didn't you answer me?"

Juana sniffed. Leah ran her hand down her arm. At the wrist, she felt the scratch of rope. Jim had tied her to the tree.

Leah grabbed the pocketknife off her belt and hacked the rope. When she finally yanked it from the tree trunk, Juana sank to the ground.

Leah put her arm around the girl's shoulder and pulled her toward her, letting her blubber into her chest, patting her like a big baby. "Did Jim tell you not to talk, is that it?"

Juana nodded.

"Then don't talk." She stood her up and brushed the needles off Juana's deerhide jacket, her thin tights. "Are you ready to go back?"

Juana nodded again.

The moon began to rise as they picked their way down to the brook and found the trail. Leah arrived at camp, teeth clenched from cold and anger, to find only BJ waiting up by the dead fire.

Geoffrey Ellis checked his e-mail, phoned Philadelphia, took a workout and steam in the Desert Paradise gym, and made his morning call to the inspector.

"Stan?"

"Nothing, sir. We've got a man down in the Casa Grande area today. Apparently this Howlin' Jim character spends a lot of time around the ruins."

"Worth a try. I realize this is not your only case."

"But it's an important one, sir."

"I appreciate your attention."

"Thank you. Now, Mister Ellis, in regards to the pottery you sent -"

"Those are for your wife."

"But sir, regulations -"

"They have nothing to do with you, Stan, or with this investigation. They're a token of my appreciation for a pleasant day, nothing more."

"Well, then, thank you."

"Don't mention it. And I mean that. Do you understand?"

"Yes, sir."

"Good. Any press snooping around?"

"None of the police reporters have picked up on it."

"And you'll see that none do. I'll call you later, Stan."

At the Desert Botanical Garden he strolled along the paved trails, watching families admire mighty saguaro and dangerous cholla, children dash from cactus to cactus. *Maybe they're here,* he thought. *Maybe they'll just show up here. Wouldn't that be something?* He searched every child's face, smiled at young parents pushing strollers and shielding their babies from the blistering autumn sun.

He studied placards describing Arizona plants—their growth patterns, locales, uses. A humble-looking bush with tiny berries caught his eye.

"…the western soapberry, found in profusion above Payson, along the Mogollon Rim…"

There it was: his password. The word Branson had given him, years ago.

He pulled out his cell phone. "They're not in Casa Grande, Stan."

"Sir?"

"I have an idea."

"What have you found, sir?"

"Nothing. It's just a hunch. You can call off your search."

"I can't just call it off. It's against regulations."

"You're the head of this investigation, aren't you? You have the authority to call it off."

"Sir, it's our duty—"

"It's your duty not to waste taxpayers' money on wild goose chases. I appreciate the discretion with which you've handled this matter. Goodbye, Stan."

He clicked off. When the phone tweedled a minute later, he was in full stride toward the entry gate, heading for his car, and didn't bother to answer. Within minutes he was speeding up the freeway toward the Desert Paradise. An hour later, he scribbled a note for the chambermaid, gifting her the many vases of tulips in his room, left a generous tip in an envelope for the gift shop girl, and checked out.

Chapter 16

Jim said they were going on a long hunt, possibly three days. Leah had been waiting for such an opportunity.

With Alissa watching, she loaded her pack with meat. She wore a hat, wool socks, vest, and jacket. Alissa pouted, near tears.

"How long is longer than usual?"

"I don't know, Liss. Just don't worry."

"You always say that. As if I'm gonna sit around worrying."

Leah stopped packing long enough to pull Alissa to her. "You're the world's bravest eight-year-old," she said, kissing the girl's dark crown. She pulled on her wool gloves. "Check the snares. Take care of BJ and Juana."

She sped along familiar routes, through the clearing, around the outcrop, across seven streams, circling the sides of the bowl. This time she would find that opening.

By now she was adept at slithering through the forest. She could be fast and quiet, stay on her route yet alert to the sounds of the woods. Too rushed for fear, she was aware of bird calls, a squirrel dropping a twig, the trickle of the next rivulet.

At the boundary of her known territory, she stopped to wolf the meat, then pressed on, barring doubt from her mind. She built hasty cairns but hardly glanced back to fix them in her memory.

At sunset, she reached a steep rock face. It was totally vertical; a few weeks ago, she would have considered it unclimbable. But this evening, with fingers numb, with no rope, and an empty stomach, she would reach the top.

About forty feet above the forest floor, she sensed a familiarity to the rocks, as if her hands and feet knew where to put themselves. She didn't look down until she hauled herself up the last overhang and sprawled on the rock, panting.

A pair of yellow eyes was watching. The coyote sat just out of her reach. She lay looking at its eyes and soft underbelly fur for some time, before sitting up.

"Hello, coyote."

It cocked its head, as dogs do.

"Did you come to tell me something?"

The coyote turned its gaze, drawing her attention to the view behind her. The vast wilderness spread below, bathed in evening light.

And she knew: this was the spot where Branson and Geoffrey had stopped to call the spirits. Just ahead would be the clearing, and then the cliff they'd skittered around in the dark.

So her theory was correct. She'd scribed a circle around the bowl. She'd found the crack.

But the trip here had taken all day, whereas on that first dark night, they'd arrived at camp within a few hours. Jim must have known a shortcut; he always did.

When she stood up, the coyote moved toward the trees and took up a new post. At the edge of the rocks the trees were so dense she had to squeeze between them sideways; she stumbled in soft pine-needle earth, ready to collapse from fatigue.

The smell of machinery reached her nostrils. She followed it.

A hundred feet later, in a tiny clearing, sprawled the Ellis backhoe they'd passed on the way in. It had been burned to a cinder. Its bucket lay on the ground like a dead animal, its skeletal lifting mechanism twisted, the tires flopped and blown. Patches of distinctive Ellis Blue were visible under a coat of oil, soot, and dust.

"Branson."

This is where he came with Geoffrey, on the day they returned to camp smelling of gasoline.

He had killed his father. He had denounced Geoffrey Ellis for making machinery for diggers to defile the ancients. Now Branson was a criminal himself, and he had made Geoffrey his accomplice. She was married to a crazy man who blew up things and was warping their son. Branson had some pieces missing, just like the pots made of shards and glue. Even if she got him out of there, even with all his family's resources, Branson might never be put back together again.

But elation pushed grief aside. She knew where she was. From here, she could find a road.

She circled the machine, inspecting every part of it in the last moments of light, touching the hard metal, the first factory-made object she'd seen in weeks.

The ground was cold, but she didn't mind. Tomorrow she was going to start putting their lives back the way they were. She would use every bit of her strength and knowledge, everything she'd learned. Tomorrow, Jim would know the power of her magic.

She scooped out a spot in the earth, making a hump for a pillow and a hollow for her hips, and slept until morning.

Despite an aching back, hands like slabs of meat, and teeth clenched against the cold, Leah opened her eyes and smiled at the sight of the rusted machine.

The backhoe, an instrument of criminals? Howlin' Jim's brainwash had tipped Branson over the edge.

And for all they knew, the backhoe didn't belong to diggers. Maybe it was a rancher's, for working his ditches. But up here, in the woods? Perhaps the rancher was also an amateur pot hunter, his blade handy for pushing down thousand-year-old walls, the shovel gouging through layers of protective dirt and dredging up treasures that were never meant to be seen. Perhaps the rancher glued shards together in his garage, then sold them to a desert rat, who sold them to a dealer, who sold them to a museum or a collector.

Then who was the criminal: The rancher? The dealer? The museum? Or Branson?

Today it wasn't an issue. Leah grinned. Today she would find a road, flag down a car. She would get to some town and get the sheriff and a rescue team, and they'd go to the camp with her. The sheriff would arrest Howlin' Jim for kidnapping. Juana would go to foster care. Branson would get therapy. Today, they would start over.

Something about the machine caught her eye. On the fender, someone had spread his hand on the burnt metal and scratched the soot around it, leaving a perfect image of the hand. In the palm sat a turquoise nugget.

It was a right hand. The artist was left-handed.

Howlin' Jim was left-handed. He must have followed her there. Leah crumpled beside the machine as if she'd been stomach-punched.

With tears streaking her dirty face, she plunged back into the woods. *Now he knows I can find the way out. What will he do to me? To Branson? The children?*

She climbed down the cliff, thrashed through the forest, with no option but to retrace her steps the long way around the bowl. Jim might be watching her even as she ran; or he may have taken his shortcut and be back in camp already.

All morning, she didn't stop. She choked down the last of the meat as she fled, paused only to fill her water bottle. By nightfall she was in familiar territory. She spotted a cairn, then another.

Finally, at Juana's father's "grave," she stumbled. She lay on the pine needles, panting, before tackling the final hill. Whatever punishment Jim had for her, she was ready. Leah struggled up the steep embankment, pulling on branches, and hauled herself onto their ledge.

The camp was gone.

Her tent, the children's, Juana's: gone. The fire circle had been dismantled. Cooking equipment, supplies, vanished.

Leah circled the area in disbelief, her mind not grasping what her eyes were seeing. Wind whistled by her ears as she wandered through the ruin, past the half-built kiva, as if she had only dreamed the family that once lived there. In the deep cave, the burial cavern lay undisturbed beneath its cover of brush and leaves. Her bowl and fetish hadn't been moved. Their home was as dead as the Mogollon.

Like a sleepwalker, she drifted into the cave where they'd built the rooms, and found Branson.

He was dozing against the wall, his expedition-sized pack propped beside him. She fell into his arms. He held her against him while she cried.

"We've moved to a new camp."

"Geoffrey and Alissa?"

"They're all right. They're worried about you."

"You let him take them away?"

"I had no choice. I'm supposed to bring you there. Are you all right? We all thought you were gone. I was afraid I'd lost you this time."

Leah dried her face on his jacket. "Why did he move?"

"He didn't say."

"Do you know where I've been?"

"No. Tell me."

"I've been, I went to—"

"Where?"

So Jim hadn't told Branson, because he knew Branson would go after her. Being so close to escape, she might persuade him to let her out. So he kept her children as hostages and moved to a new hideout.

Branson stroked her hair. "Don't worry, Leah."

"Don't worry."

"We have to go to the kids now."

"I can't move. I've been walking for two days."

"Then rest a while."

He gave her some dried meat and a few nuts. Lying in his arms like a deflated balloon, she could hardly swallow the food. Branson stared into the dusk, as if listening to someone speaking in the forest.

"Branson, I found something."

He waited.

"Actually, it was nothing."

"What did you find?"

"I can't be an ancient, Branson. How can I make you understand this is not going to work for me? This is what you wanted. This was all your choice, not mine."

"So you were looking for your magic, but you didn't find it."

"I didn't find anything."

"I'm glad you tried. I haven't found mine yet, either. I understand."

No, you don't understand. The days of our understanding each other are over. I can't tell you about the backhoe. I can't tell you about the skeleton lying just a few hundred yards from here. You're weak and you're crazy. I can't tell you anything.

He stood up, stretching. "Can you walk now?"

"I think so."

He shouldered his huge backpack. They set out in darkness, with no moon to show the way. Leah followed one step behind Branson. He accommodated her pace, holding branches aside and helping her over boulders.

How can the woods be so big? How can we go any deeper?

When she had to stop, Branson spread their sleeping bag beneath an overhanging rock. She climbed inside, her teeth chattering, legs quivering. In the moment before she slept, she glimpsed the cold, starry sky and wondered how long it would be until she, like Branson, went mad.

❖ ❖ ❖ ❖ ❖

All the next day, he coaxed her over rocks, down gullies, across streams.

Every place they went looked like every other place, blurring in Leah's mind with the days before. A deep hopelessness overtook her as she trudged behind Branson.

At nightfall they entered a clearing. Leah saw an uneven circle of tents. There was a fire ring, stumps for seats, the dog. BJ was poking at the fire; Juana drooped around her tent.

Alissa ran sobbing to Leah and clung as if she were drowning. Despite Jim's sharp look, Geoffrey dropped the water gourds and ran to his mother. Juana and BJ threw themselves at her, wailing. Leah sat on the ground and hugged them all.

She exchanged looks with Jim. Her look told him what he wanted to know: that she had not told Branson about finding the backhoe. And Jim's, in exchange, told her she could her keep her family.

It was their secret. Only she knew why Jim had brought them to this place.

❖ ❖ ❖ ❖ ❖

The new camp was dreadful. There was no cave and only a small, exposed ruin. Water was far away. There was no ponderosa forest, only low junipers that afforded little protection from sun and wind.

BJ had moved her stuff back into the tiny tent with Juana. Neither she nor Jim mentioned it.

At breakfast Jim said, "We don't need a cave. We'll build pithouses. The Sinagua used them for centuries before they moved into caves."

Nobody responded. Juana stood in her patchwork deerskin, glaring. BJ looked puzzled and hurt.

"Can't mix adobe in this cold," Leah croaked, too tired to mount a real protest.

"The last place was better," said Alissa.

"Ge'h."

Leah hadn't the strength or the will to supervise the activities of the women. Her vow to escape seemed long ago, like a dream from childhood. All day she lay in her tent, with Alissa sleeping beside her, holding her hand.

When she went out in the evening, she found Juana hunched by the fire, and BJ making an absurd effort to haul rocks.

Juana looked up. "This sucks."

BJ dropped her load of rocks and rubbed the girl's shoulders. "If you'd put some effort in, it would be better."

Juana shrugged her off. "Screw effort. I hate this camp."

"It's up to us to make it work."

"I don't give a shit."

BJ sat down, looking to Leah for help. Leah couldn't muster the energy to stop their squabbling.

BJ's clothes hung in tatters, filthy and ridiculous. She was still wearing Jim's bloody, mud-colored jacket. It fit her like a mattress. Leah couldn't think of a thing to say.

Chapter 17

Geoffrey Ellis sped toward Payson, an unpretentious town nestled at the foot of the Mogollon Rim. In many aspects Payson was like other western towns, with its strip of motels and fast foods and stores; but its frontier history was evident in hewn-wood signs and log architecture that gave a nod to its pioneer past. As he approached, he saw the Rim rise behind the town—wooded, yet steep, sheltering, solid.

He took two rooms at a motel, one for him and one for his maps, and found a restaurant.

"Who's the ranger around here?" he asked the waitress as she returned the change from his hundred-dollar bill.

"That'd be Vern Crouse. They live out next to the forest station, edge of town." She pointed east.

"Thank you. And tell the chef that salad was outstanding."

"He'll be glad to hear it. Whatcha need Vern for?"

"Some research I'm doing." Geoffrey Ellis picked up his receipt, leaving the money on the table, and stood to leave.

Her eyes widened as she looked at the pile of change. "Uh, sir—"

"It's for you. You're a good waitress. Good night."

He phoned the ranger station from his room. Introducing himself as Jeff Ellis, he made an appointment for the next morning with Vern Crouse. The ranger was a large, comfortable man who'd lived in the Mogollon area all his life, and was now looking forward to retirement, to spend more time outdoors.

"Been behind a desk too long," he said, during their initial pleasantries. "Wanta get out there and work off some of this." He patted his stomach, which strained the buttons on his tan ranger's shirt. "Get back to why I started in this business in the first place."

"And why was that?"

"The Rim got hold of me, I guess, like it can do. The woods, the ruins, the history. You seen Shoofly Village yet?"

"What's that?"

"Prehistoric excavation, just up that bench. Worth a visit. Gives you a pretty good idea what life was like back then. Now, what can I help you with, Jeff?"

Geoffrey Ellis surveyed the topographic maps that covered every wall of the ranger's office. They were arrayed so that, starting on the left wall, the convoluted Rim could be traced in detail, west to east, along its two hundred-mile length.

"This is all your territory?"

"'Fraid so," Vern laughed. "Of course, most of the activity's concentrated in the recreation spots. Campgrounds, fishing, hunting. People can go up there all their lives and never leave civilization. But a lot of what you see here is untracked, so nobody goes in those parts."

"Like which parts?"

"Well," Vern stood up and indicated a vast section to the east. "This is the Tonto Wilderness. I've never gone very far into there myself. Always wanted to."

Vern's wife appeared at the door with a tray and two cups of coffee, which she'd brought over from the house. "Knock, knock," she said. "Cream and sugar, Jeff? None for you, Vern."

"Black, thanks. You're very kind."

"She takes good care of me," Vern smiled. "She's the reason our son decided to stick around this neck of the woods."

His wife laughed. "That's not true. Vern has been his inspiration since he was a little boy."

Vern chuckled. "He didn't want to lose out on his mother's cooking, that's the real reason. He's in forestry school now. You have kids, Jeff?"

Geoffrey Ellis leaned forward on his chair. He was accustomed to deference and respect, and the ranger's easy manner threw him off. "Well, Vern, that's what I've come to see you about."

And he started to cry.

They spent an hour together. Vern rubbed his chin and nodded while Geoffrey Ellis told him his suspicions about what had happened. He didn't question that a whole family could vanish into the woods, because he'd met his share of unbalanced people; and he didn't judge, because he could see the pain on the man's face. He got out a large roll of tracing paper and taped it over the maps. With a marker he crosshatched the populated sections that had roads, campgrounds, and tourist areas. With another color he marked all the known prehistoric ruins. The exercise cut the search area to a more manageable size. Over the untracked wilderness, he scribbled a big green question mark.

"Here's the area I'd say we should start with," he said. "My boy's coming this afternoon. I bet he'd like nothing more than to hit the backcountry this weekend. Would you be up for that, Jeff?"

As Geoffrey Ellis walked to his car, he experienced his first hint of hope since arriving in Arizona. Tears still welled inside him, but they were tears of relief. He had an immediate goal: buy some hiking boots, a pack, and a warm jacket. And he had a team.

Watching him leave, Vern said to his wife, "Did you put it together who Jeff Ellis is?"

"Yes. He's a man who loves his son."

BJ was trying to raise Leah's spirits. "Hey," she called. "Let's go get some pure Arizona spring water." She tossed Leah a gourd and started out of the pitiful camp.

There wasn't even a hint of a trail. There was no view, no magic. Instead of mourning for the life she left so long ago, Leah mourned the caves and her buried ancient. The world here was made of trees and sorrow.

BJ led the way over logs and rocks, ducking branches, with Leah straggling behind, not caring.

"Here's the spring."

"This?"

"It's not Niagara Falls, you understand."

Water drizzled out of the ground, turning the hillside to muck. Leah studied it with bitterness at the thought that they were now forced to eke their water from this lousy source—and that it was her fault.

"Let's dig a basin so we can dip the gourd."

They scooped out a pile of mud and lined the cut with pebbles, creating a tiny pool. Even so, the flow was so weak it was difficult to fill the gourds without dirt getting in.

Leah sat. "Well, this is a pain in the butt."

BJ stared at her for a moment. Instead of cracking a joke or sending her a smile, she picked at the mud drying under her fingernails and raked a springy lock of hair off her forehead. Even BJ couldn't stay cheery forever.

"Leah, I have something to show you. You won't tell, will you?"

"What do you think?"

"Okay, follow me." BJ headed deeper into the trees.

They crawled under thick brush along the face of a dark outcrop, sometimes squirming over the forest floor. BJ pulled aside a branch to reveal a horizontal slit in the rock. She slithered inside.

Leah followed on her belly. The cave was just big enough to curl up in. She lay next to BJ and looked at her dark eyes glinting in the dim light of the opening.

"My hidey-hole," said BJ.

"And why do you need a hidey-hole?"

"Just—if I should want to be alone. Whatever. Like it?"

"Better call a decorator. It's a bit dark."

"You think anybody could find it?"

"Anybody?"

"Like Jim."

"Oh, please. Jim can find anything."

BJ sighed and turned away.

"What, BJ? You need to hide from Jim?"

"Just sometimes."

"Oh, damn."

"I mean, just sometimes, you know. Not always."

The men were waiting when they got back. Leah and BJ scurried around, starting the fire, skinning the game. Leah found her way around the new kitchen, aware that Jim was watching her. He sat at the fire while she worked, not speaking.

Juana approached him with the vest she'd been working on. Even given it was her first attempt, it was awful: patchy, full of clumsy seams and knots. Leah held her breath.

"What's that?"

"It's a vest for you."

Jim stared at the fire. "Chodistaas," he said to BJ. "I'm cold. Bring me my blanket."

BJ hurried to him with the skin blanket, laid it over his shoulders, and slipped away.

"You could try on your new vest," said Juana. "You could see if it fits." She no longer held the thing out to him, just slumped with her arms at her sides.

Jim looked into the woods. "Now I understand why there's no progress on the pithouses. Why there are no stones gathered, no adobe started. This is what you do all day instead of working, wasting your time on this travesty."

"It's for you, Jim."

He swatted the vest out of her hands. "You're learning nothing. You're wasting skins."

Juana tried to leave, but he caught her by the ankle.

"Don't waste any more time or resources. From now on, you carry rocks, water, and firewood. Nothing else. Understood?"

Leah thought, *You've got all your animals in their cages, haven't you, Jim? Even I am too tired to intervene for Juana this time.*

Branson looked as if he might say something, but didn't. The others let it pass. Juana sat on the log. She didn't pick up the vest, didn't attempt a retort.

Oh, yes. You have all your animals. Juana has killed her father and has nobody else. Branson killed his father, and he brought you Geoffrey, as proof of his loyalty.

Jim stirred the fire. "Where's that meat?"

Then there's BJ. What zookeeper wouldn't be proud of a beautiful, pliant specimen like BJ? She's loyal to death and denies her own intelligence. Alissa, no more of a challenge than Chaco; she doesn't eat much, and she'll be useful one day.

"It's ready."

"Give it to me now."

Okay, Jim. The meat is yours. You don't even have to be charming or persuasive anymore. Everything is yours. You've got it all, for now.

Everything but me. I'm going to get my strength back, and then you'll have to deal with me again.

A few days later, rested and fed, Leah decided to challenge Jim.

When the men came in early from hunting, she said, "Branson's going to take Alissa and me for a little hike, to show us around the area. We'll set some snares."

Jim laid his bow against the wall and took a long drink. He still wore only a thin shirt. He had cut the terrible vest apart and used the skins for game bags.

Leah pulled Branson's hand, watching Howlin' Jim. "Come on, let's go."

"Branson." Jim wasn't looking at them. "Leave the girl."

Leah said, "We're taking her."

Jim picked up his things and walked to his sleeping place behind the wall. Leah caught Branson's look of doubt, almost fear.

"Damn it, she's coming." She stalked into the forest, pulling Alissa by the hand.

Once away from camp, Branson began to relax. He showed them a minuscule ruin under a rock, which ancients had built for an emergency shelter. The vegetation around their new site was even more difficult to move through than the ponderosa forest. Branson explained that, on the Rim, only north-facing slopes supported fir and pine, and that junipers and Douglas firs lived in a reverse of normal climate zones.

Leah laughed. "Always the professor."

"It's good to hear you laugh."

"How could I ever have been annoyed by your lecturing?"

Alissa tugged Branson's hand. "Tell us some more professor stuff."

"You're just trying to get me to talk."

"Yeah." Alissa grinned. "It's not like you're a bag of chuckles these days, Dad."

He grabbed her by the ribs and began to tickle her. "We'll see who's a bag of chuckles. Feel that? No? What about this?"

Alissa squealed and squirmed out of his grasp. "You gotta catch me! Come on, I dare you!"

Branson pretended to chase her through the junipers, with Leah laughing behind him. They ran until the three of them fell into a heap.

Wind shrieked through the trees like ancient voices. They crowded into a small cave, Alissa in Branson's lap.

"I like just us alone, like this," she mumbled into his chest. "Do you, Dad?"

"Sure, Liss. It's nice."

"Why can't we bring Geoffrey, too? Why can't we take a picnic some-times? Why do you have to go away every day?"

They stayed in the cave until dusk, not talking much, just clinging to-gether and enjoying their own company. Leah felt like a battery on trickle charge, absorbing strength from Branson—though not enough to jump-start her own engine.

When hunger drove them back to camp, they saw Jim by the fire with Geoffrey, teaching him something about arrow points. He didn't look up.

❖ ❖ ❖ ❖ ❖

Immediately after eating, Juana retreated to her tent.

Leah scratched on the tent wall. "Hey, Juana, you okay?"

"Beat it."

Back at the fire, she said, "Where's BJ?"

Geoffrey nodded toward the spring.

Leah stared into the darkness. "I'd better go see."

"Leave her," said Jim.

"She might need help."

"I said leave her. Go be with your husband."

In their tent, Branson whispered, "This morning she told me that if she didn't come back, you'd know where she was."

Leah hoped BJ's hidey-hole was cozy.

In the morning BJ had the fire going early, a pot of water boiling, the willow-bark tea simmering. Her sleeping bag was airing on the low wall.

"You're a bright one today," Leah commented.

Jim stepped into the fire circle. "Chodistaas. Bring your sleeping bag."

BJ's smile vanished.

Leah whispered, "You don't have to go, BJ. Just tell him you don't want to."

"I can't do that. I brought this on myself."

"You did not."

"I bought into it, Leah. You didn't. That's the difference between you and me."

"BJ, stop. You don't have to."

"Chodistaas." The threat in Jim's voice had ratcheted up a notch. He set his cup onto the fire ring and stood watching her.

BJ picked up the bag and trudged behind him into the juniper woods.

A few minutes later Jim returned, poured a cup of tea, and drank it standing up. BJ emerged from the trees, her clothes hanging like sails on a ghost ship. She appeared to be walking with difficulty, and her eyes would not meet Leah's.

Jim picked up his bow and quiver. "Women who leave without permission are foolish. They should be available if needed. Branson, Kaibito, are you ready?"

Chapter 18

Leah couldn't get a word out of BJ—not a complaint or even an opinion. She wouldn't smile, wouldn't crack a joke. She did her work, walked out to clear the snares, brought water and stones for the pithouse; but she was a gray presence. This dull, vague drudge was a BJ Leah had never known. Like Juana, she spent as much time as possible lying in her tent.

Leah already had too much to worry about. She watched Branson contradict Jim more often. He seemed to be digging a chasm between them, seeking ways to demonstrate his independence and challenge Jim—much as he had once created the gulf between himself and his father. But this distancing was coming fast, whereas it took years for Branson to make the break from Geoffrey Ellis. Jim's distrust of Branson's growing competence was obvious. Though they hunted together and made no overt change to their routine, Leah sensed the animosity beneath the surface. Jim had preached that the group couldn't survive without cooperation from every one of its members. Leah believed it. She used to fear the men's friendship and wished to wedge them apart. Now she was getting her wish, and she feared it.

She watched Geoffrey follow Jim in silence, absorbing his teachings, as Branson had done before. He had moved into the place of favor once occupied by his father. Leah's guilt over her part in bringing them all to this awful new home prevented her from gaining control over her son's allegiance, even in camp.

Juana was just impossible. If Leah had more energy, she might have attempted to salve the big girl's hurt or at least get some work out of her. But she watched helplessly as the Juana shrank farther into her anger and refused to participate.

Even bright-star Alissa had lost her luster. Undernourished like the rest of them, she played alone, singing to herself, and no longer took pride in leading the women through the woods or bringing in birds from the snares.

Despite the odds, Leah still had faint hope for a rebellion. She didn't know how, or when; but she dreamed of throwing open the cages and leading an insurrection.

With constant hunger and despondent troops, her hope grew fainter each day. And, she feared, Jim was still planning her punishment. She looked for signs whenever she caught his eyes. He kept aloof, speaking to her only when necessary.

One afternoon as she worked on the watercourse for the little spring, Jim materialized out of the juniper brush. His face was painted yellow and black.

"Damn it, Jim. Jump out at the deer, not me."

To her surprise, he smiled. "Sorry."

The smile and apology were the last things she expected. She looked at him: his light eyes glinted, his hair was freshly braided, a pair of red feathers woven in. He smelled as if he'd just washed.

"Why did you paint today?"

"You'll know soon."

She continued working on the spring. She had made a half-pipe of yucca basketry, pinning it at the opening with four sharpened sticks, to conduct the water a few inches away from the side of the hill so the gourd could fit under it.

"Good," said Jim, examining the spout.

Now it comes, she thought. *He can be very creative in his punishments. Okay, Jim, dish it out.*

He untied his medicine bundle and handed her a forked twig wrapped tightly with alternating blue and yellow threads. He pointed to a little wad of feathers adorning the end, tied with red thread. "This is from your sleeping bag."

"You cut it off our sleeping bag?"

"It's a man-stick."

"You went into our tent and cut it off our bag?"

"It was necessary. You haven't gotten pregnant."

She jumped up. "You're out of your mind! I can't believe you're still on that track!" She started to leave, but his hard hand caught hers and pulled her down.

"Stay still. I'm not going to hurt you."

He took out a tiny pipe, its stem a hollow bone, the bowl an acorn, and packed it with a pinch of leaves. Striking his flints, he ignited a handful of grass and lit the pipe, then gave it to her.

"Hold your man-stick over your heart. Inhale."

"No."

"It's a request, not an order."

Leah sighed and sucked the bone stem. Her lungs and head filled with sweet essence.

"Again."

He grasped the hand that held the prayer stick and pressed it to her chest as she took another draw. Her eyes blurred. She gave in to the pressure of his palm.

"You continue to defy me, with all your strength. I want to harness that strength. I need your help. I need your influence."

"My influence."

"I want to give you more magic. With your intuition, and what I can give you, you'll be even stronger."

From somewhere far away, she saw herself reaching for the pipe, craving another cloud of its sweet smoke in her lungs. When she released the smoke, it felt as if Jim were sucking the breath out of her. She saw Jim's hand open her jacket and find her breast, saw herself relax into his grasp, making no effort to escape his touch.

His beard scratched her neck. He whispered, "Even with your strength, I can resist you. I can be this close and still resist you. Branson's weak. He can't."

"Branson?"

"You're using his weakness to turn him against me."

She heard herself laugh, a harsh, faraway sound. "You own Branson."

"You know what you're doing, and so do I."

"If I could do what you think, we'd be visiting the ancients in the museum, where they belong. I wouldn't have to steal corn from them to feed my kid." Leah giggled. Something she'd just said was very clever, but she couldn't remember what it was. This was some good stuff she was smoking.

She felt his hand withdraw, felt him sit up. "What do you mean?" he said.

"Mean?" I'm not mean, you are." She giggled again.

"About stealing corn from the ancients."

Oh, damn. That's what she'd said that was so clever. She sat up. "We gotta smoke that pipe more often, Jim. Makes life in the woods a lot more interesting."

"What corn did you steal from the ancients?"

"Just a figure of speech."

"I don't believe you."

She coughed. What the hell was she doing? Jim was her enemy. He tied girls to trees. He made her best friend hide in a cave. Why was she smoking with him, letting him touch her?

Lights buzzed around her face as she stood up. She couldn't get any words out. Jim didn't try to stop her or keep her there. He looked far away, an Indian crouched by a stream in some other time, some other country, through the wrong end of a telescope. She clawed her way up the hill, scraping her cheek on a low branch.

She turned back to look. He still squatted beside the spring, staring at her. His eyes glinted like polished stones. Even underneath the paint, she could see his expression. It was the scowl of a spurned, suspicious lover.

That night, Branson was helping Geoffrey trim down his bow and re-string it at a shorter length, to better fit his body and the dense brush where they did most of their hunting now.

Jim, who had not looked at Leah since she left him at the spring, took the bow from Geoffrey to examine it. "Not like that," he said. "You'll lose the balance."

Branson stood up. "I did it this way on mine."

"Kaibito, you have to take down both ends and make two new notches. Stop what you're doing and unstring the other end."

Branson took the bow from Jim. "I say let him try it like this for a day. If it doesn't work, he can change it."

"And possibly miss his target as a result."

"It works fine for me."

"We can't afford to miss even one shot."

"You haven't seen me miss many shots, have you? Leave it, Kaibito."

Geoffrey, uncomfortable, finished trimming and stringing the bow as Branson instructed. Jim muttered "Ge'h" and disappeared into the woods. The next day Geoffrey shot a young deer; but neither he nor Branson exulted. Jim hung in the shadow while they skinned the animal and cooked the meat.

Leah became extra alert to the men's interactions. Jim's coolness increased. And Branson seemed to tweak him intentionally, like a teenager bugging his father. Leah worried. Howlin' Jim was no gruff-but-indulgent Geoffrey Ellis.

When Jim outlined his plan for the men's kiva, Branson challenged him again. "We should finish the shelters first."

"Women will build the pithouses."

"They can't work fast enough by themselves."

"We'll stay in the tents, then. The kiva is paramount."

Branson backed down. *He still values his place in the company of men,* Leah thought. But his passive-aggressive maneuvers were easy to observe, under their simple living circumstances.

Was he contemplating a move, to dethrone Jim and claim leadership? Leah doubted it; still, the men's unspoken rivalry lay like a crocodile under the surface of a swamp. They rarely laughed or talked. They both instructed Geoffrey, using their words to him to convey warnings to one another—and, Leah knew, putting Geoffrey in a terrible position.

Jim continued to insist on the "natural" practice of separating men and women. He worked on the kiva and glowered if Branson didn't move fast enough. He slept alone in the unfinished kiva—unless it was a mating night, when he summoned BJ to join him in the cold juniper brush.

Toward Leah, Branson would be companionable one day, remote the next. *Jim believes I'm using my power over Branson,* Leah thought. *But I have none. This is how Branson's always been, equivocal and conflicted. Okay, call it weak. Branson listens to too many voices.*

In their tent she whispered, "Jim's jealous of you."

He turned his back. "When you speak against him, you undercut our organization."

"You're mouthing his words. Have you forgotten how to speak for yourself?"

"We can't afford to be petty."

"In a matter of weeks, we've reverted a thousand years. That's hardly petty."

"We've escaped. Not reverted."

"We still have emotions. The ancients had emotions. Even Jim has them, and his emotion is jealousy. He's even trying to steal Geoffrey."

Guilty, yet protective of Branson as always, she hadn't mentioned her encounters with Jim in the woods, his soft flattery and obvious overtures. Best not to toss that snake into the pit.

Branson stirred. "Kaibito's my son. Jim knows he can't steal him. He's concerned for our survival, so he's teaching him."

Leah sighed. "Branson, please take us back. I can't stand this anymore."

He turned and pulled her to him. His beard smelled of fire and blood and game, smells that were her world now.

"You can stand it," he said. "Think how far you've come. Think of everything you can do now, that you'd never have believed yourself capable of."

She squirmed beneath his sinewy arms. Even though he curled his body protectively around her, she knew he couldn't choose her over Jim.

In her mind, she heard herself saying goodbye. Hope was gone. Grief would come later.

Branson said, "We can't go back. We've changed too much."

Geoffrey Ellis was glad to be in motion. He spent the weekend combing the edge of the Rim with Vern Crouse and his son. Their search came up dry, but at least they were taking action.

They would drive in as far as possible, then hike along separate trails until a designated turn-around time, and reconvene at the truck. They questioned the few people they encountered—hunters scouting routes in advance of the coming season, and the occasional out-of-state tourist—but no one had sighted the group.

Sunday night, in the little house next to the ranger station, Vern finished off his wife's pot roast and pushed his chair back from the table. "Well, Jeff, I'm sorry to say I have to go back to work tomorrow."

"You don't know how much I appreciate what you've done."

Geoffrey Ellis was already thinking of how to repay them. But for once, laying an expensive gift on them wasn't the thing to do. Vern and his wife were—he struggled with an unaccustomed idea—friends.

Vern looked vexed. "If we had evidence they're in the area, I'd call for help in an official capacity. But as it is…"

"I know. Hunches don't count." *Although my hunch was enough for you to give me your weekend,* he thought.

"Heard anything from Phoenix?"

"The only name that keeps coming up is the Howlin' Jim character, but it leads nowhere. There doesn't seem to be any ID on the guy, although a lot of people agree he exists."

Vern scratched his head. "Puff of smoke."

"In my world, Vern, we don't believe in puffs of smoke. But I'm getting the idea things work differently out here."

The men had marked their forays on the maps in Vern's office. Standing back to study the scribbles, Geoffrey Ellis was awed by how much territory remained, much of it without road or trail. And knowing firsthand, now, how an innocuous set of lines on the map could translate into deep brush, impassible marsh, or heart-stopping cliffs, he appreciated the task before them.

Vern accepted a sliver of pie from his wife. "So you'll head back in alone."

"Yes. I'll take you up on that offer of a tent, if you don't mind."

"Sure. How about a sleeping bag?"

"Got one already, thanks."

"Nights can get long out there."

"They're long in the motel."

"They can get cold."

"You're not trying to talk me out of it, are you, Vern?"

He set out before dawn in the SUV he'd bought. He followed Crook's Trail east but eventually abandoned it, on a whim, for a path that led into the deep ponderosa. There were pockets of snow in the shadows, but the morning was bright; it felt like a day for discovery.

Eventually he had to park the car. He'd scraped the undercarriage several times, steering over downed trees and rocks that lurked beneath the pine needles. He used his cell phone to check his messages one last time, struggled into his backpack, and set off on foot.

Two hours later, he dumped the pack and ate the sandwich Mrs. Crouse had sent. His shoulders ached. He'd seen nothing but trees.

I haven't been alone in the woods since I was a Boy Scout. He stretched out and let the sun warm his face. The sounds of the forest came to him: twigs dropping, wind, a skittering squirrel.

Slowly, Geoffrey Ellis began to grasp the idea of lost. Though certain he could find the car, he still felt prickliness creep under his skin—fear, almost, as if his body were warning him.

He moved on, tying fluorescent ribbon markers on branches. *I would get lost without these, no question about it.* Still, he thought with surprise, *I like it here.* Then he added, quite honestly, *I'm scared.*

At dusk, he was so tired he forgot his fear. He set up Vern's tent, lighted the little camp stove, and heated water for freeze-dried stew. *Am I crazy, or is this delicious?*

An owl hoo-hooed. Little creatures scampered. He turned off the whirring stove and let the sounds settle around him. He'd covered a lot of Rim today: dense forests, cliffs with wide vistas, brush he had to hack through.

He sipped his cocoa, thinking that if he died there, it would be a long time before Vern found him. The thought was not at all frightening.

If they came here, they died here.

He reviewed that last thought. Yes, if they did come here, they certainly they were dead.

All those years I worried about the children being kidnapped, the bodyguards I hired to protect them. And now it has happened. There wasn't a thing I could do. Geoffrey Ellis drew a circle with his flashlight, moving it from tree to tree. The beam picked out a pair of eyes; it was a deer, twig in its mouth.

He shivered, stood, and urinated against a tree. He thought about how his days came and went in the wingbeat of a moth, but nights were endless. Tonight could be a record breaker.

Branson, I wanted you to be happy, to find something right and resonant in your life, as I did.

He crawled into his sleeping bag. He swallowed his nighttime pills with water from his bottle and put his jacket into the stuff sack to make a pillow, as the salesman had shown him.

That wasn't the whole story, the complete truth, he admitted. He had wanted Branson to be happy, sure; but he also wanted to be proud of him. But Branson wouldn't give him that.

Unlike his sisters, Branson had never done anything for Geoffrey Ellis to brag about. Whatever his father wanted, Branson did the opposite.

Maybe I should've let you follow your passion. But then you would have left me even sooner. Maybe I should've sent you to a good boarding school, taught you some discipline. Maybe I was too strict. Or too lenient. Who the hell knows?

He took a last look around his campsite before zipping up the tent.

They're dead, he thought.

He stretched out and listened to the forest.

This is futile. This is dangerous. But what else can I do? What else do I have to do?

He was asleep before the next thought came.

❖   ❖   ❖   ❖   ❖

Leah lay in her tent, listening to Branson's soft snore, trying to match her breath to his.

A dream came. She was standing backstage with her children, watching Geoffrey Ellis address a packed auditorium. As the crowd stood for an ovation, Mister Ellis signaled Branson to join him on the podium.

Branson was a child, younger than Alissa. He hurried across the stage. Geoffrey Ellis lifted the boy and held him up, and the audience went wild. Branson struggled, but his father continued to hold him up for the applause. When he finally released him, the red-faced boy ran off stage.

Geoffrey Ellis turned to watch him exit. His face was painted yellow and black.

Chapter 19

Three hawks circled above the camp. Their shrieks could mean they'd spotted game. To Leah, the hawks looked like doom.

She walked out of camp beside the men. "Goodbye," she whispered to their retreating backs.

Branson moved like a robot. Jim said nothing to him, but was walking with Geoffrey, already instructing.

She mourned their leaving. She mourned the loss of her magic. She grieved for her ancient skeleton, and her bowl and fetish, back in the cave. Their old camp, with its familiar, protective walls and the rooms they'd been so proud of building, seemed like a lost paradise.

Other than sorrow, she felt only guilt.

Because of her, they had been forced to move to this foul camp. Her rashness had made them all prisoners. If she'd taken it slower, tried harder to become an ancient, made more effort to understand Branson, instead of wasting time trying to escape—if only, if only. Her regret grew stronger than her instinct to survive.

BJ watched the men disappear. "How long this time?"

"Three days, I'll bet," said Juana. "The deer are getting smarter."

"Their sense of smell improves in cold weather."

"I'm already hungry."

And so they went through their routines. Alissa was in charge of bringing in birds, but her light had dimmed, and she marched mechanically through the forest, like her father.

Juana generally refused to work. "Screw that. It's too cold."

"Come on, Juana, it'll be fun," Leah or BJ would urge; but neither of them believed it would be fun.

"Jim says all I'm good for is hauling rocks. Maybe I'm no good for that, either."

She went to her tent, looking like a rag doll on its way to the dumpster. Her face was unwashed, her hair uncombed. Her rump-sprung tights sagged at the knees and ankles.

Leah swallowed. Juana simply wouldn't work. Leah didn't dare criticize her to Jim; who knew what he might do? The rest of them would just have to do Juana's work for her. *Keep it going,* she chanted inside her head. *Get out of your tent. Haul water. Get food. The women need you.*

"Do you miss anything?" Leah asked one night, watching the little bird carcasses roast on their spits.

"Nope," Juana said. "This place sucks, but it beats the shit out of Camp Verde."

"You don't miss anybody? Boyfriend?"

Juana's laugh wasn't really a laugh. "With a father like mine?"

"Didn't you have a school counselor, Social Services—?"

"You're dumber than you look, Princess." Juana threw her stick with the charred ground squirrel into the flames and stalked to her tent.

Leah rescued Juana's dinner, to give her later.

"I miss my teacher," said Alissa.

BJ pulled her little bird out of the fire and blew on it. "To tell the truth," she said.

"To tell the truth."

"It's a little harder out here than I expected. Jim's kind of rough sometimes. I mean, he's sort of hard to be with."

Leah stared at her. "Is he hurting you?" she mouthed, so Alissa wouldn't hear.

BJ murmured, "He's pissed because I'm not pregnant."

Leah turned to Alissa. "Will you run get my wool cap, Liss? Thanks." When the child had skipped off, she said, "BJ, you're half starved, for one thing."

"He says if I'd give up my past—"

"Hey, BJ, was your past all that evil?"

"Well, I don't know. Maybe."

"Do you want a baby?"

"I used to."

"Do you?"

"I want this to work, Leah. I've never done anything important before. I just cruised along, had everything handed to me, one shallow victory after another."

"So, you need bad things to feel good?"

"I need substance. I need character."

Leah snorted. "I think you've got plenty of character, BJ."

"This is the first stand I've ever taken."

"And?"

"But Jim's not who I thought."

"I've been waiting for you to say that, but hearing it doesn't give me pleasure."

"He's brilliant and fascinating, yeah, but sometimes he's a little scary." BJ's dark eyes shone in the firelight. She laughed. "Man, I sure know how to pick 'em, don't I?"

"You get the prize."

Alissa came back with Leah's cap. She stood by her mother, breaking twigs and tossing them into the fire. Leah and BJ watched the flames. "That's entertainment," said BJ.

"I miss my bike," said Alissa.

Jim's next attempt to procreate was impossible to ignore.

Leah shook Branson awake. "Listen."

BJ's groans and muffled squeals came from behind the wall, Jim's voice—not the soothing, seductive tone Leah remembered from her meeting with him in the woods—had awakened her, deep in the night.

"What do you think?" said Leah.

"It's probably okay. They can get pretty lively."

But Leah worried. Was BJ having fun at the party?

Much later, in the dark hours before sunrise, BJ scratched on the side of their tent.

Leah unzipped the door and pulled her inside, sleeping bag and all. BJ crawled between them like a kid with a bad dream, crying. They held her, hugged her, patted her, rocked her, until the sobbing subsided.

"I'm so sorry. I hurt. I'm sorry to wake you, Branson. May I stay here?"

"Shh, BJ, just be still."

"It really hurts this time, Leah."

"Sleep now."

In the light of dawn, BJ drifted off. Leah watched her friend's troubled face, lined and haggard, a frown marring the beautiful forehead. She stared at Branson. A muscle twitched on Branson's temple—his anger muscle.

"You've got to do something, Branson."

When the sun rose, Branson crouched inside the tent as if hunting, eyes riveted on the fire circle. He looked like an ancient. His dark hair had grown almost to his shoulders, his beard soft and thick. He wore his hunting skin, a pronghorn hide layered over his jacket, to mask the smell of man.

How different he was now. His legs and arms had hardened to the texture of rope. Hands like clamps, hands that had to be reminded how to touch gently. His feet were so callused he could walk barefoot over the forest floor.

Howlin' Jim appeared at the circle, observing the unlit fire, the unboiled water. Chaco snuffled for scraps. Branson bolted from the tent, straightened, then walked toward Jim. The men exchanged a word and left camp together.

Leah started breakfast. Geoffrey and Alissa straggled in, greeted her with hugs, and sat down with their tea. She threaded strips of meat onto their sticks for them to cook, divided her own portion of piñon nuts, and added them to theirs.

Jim and Branson emerged from the trees, silent.

Geoffrey swallowed the nuts and stood ready. Jim picked up his bow and medicine bundle. He caught Leah's eyes but didn't hold them.

Branson lifted Alissa over his head, set her down, and patted her hair as she clung to his waist. He laid his hand on Leah's cheek, then shot his eyes over to the tent where BJ slept.

"Take care of her. And yourself."

She kissed his hand. The men were gone.

At Geoffrey Ellis' camp, Vern's tent sagged under a thin glaze. Geoffrey Ellis poked at the walls from inside, watching the ice crack and slide off.

He had his maps and compass, his trail of ribbons tied to trees; he knew where he was. It was comforting to pinpoint his spot on the vast Rim. Where he was headed was the question.

While his water heated, he studied the map and decided to continue east, at a level about a hundred feet below the lip of the Rim, where the contour lines indicated less steep terrain. They certainly weren't up here, on top. By picking a specific level and sticking to it, his search would be more directed. As always, he was more confident with a narrowed focus.

When he left camp, his shoulders remembered why he'd been eager to stop the previous evening. The weight of the big pack, with stove, sleeping bag, and tent, was agony. After the first mile, his muscles surrendered and his breath came easier. By mid-day he was thinking about nothing but the ponderosa and the endless rise of cliff beside him.

At sunset he felt far away from anything he'd ever known. He wanted to talk to someone. Vern, maybe. But his phone picked up no signal.

He wasn't afraid now. With all his pink ribbons tied to trees, he wouldn't get lost; and he had enough food for another day. *This must be how those prehistoric people felt,* he thought, dumping his pack and sitting for a few minutes before creaking to his feet to set up camp. *Lonely, I'll bet, but not afraid. Wherever they went, they were home.*

He got some freeze-dried food going on the stove, built a little fire for warmth. *I'm starting to understand. It all reduces to a few elements. Search, eat, sleep.*

As he crawled into his tent, he thought, *Branson, if not for you, I'd never have come here. I'd never have gotten out of my greenhouse, my office.*

He had embarked on a trip with no end in sight. If he didn't find anything this time, he'd come back, and back again. This trip would be the new definition of his life—this forest, these rock walls.

Branson, even if you're dead, I thank you for this.

Day three was turnaround day. If nothing happened by noon, he had to start back toward Payson. Once again he strapped on the pack and forced his feet to take their first steps.

The area was heavily timbered, making a set course impossible. He struggled around trunks and over logs, keeping his eyes to the ground.

Turning south, where he had seen slivers of sky behind the trees, he found himself atop a cliff. The forest lay below like a safety net beneath the edge of the world. Far to the south, the desert moonscape shimmered, brown and glinting.

It was too early to turn back, but there was nowhere to go. Geoffrey Ellis sat on the edge, legs hanging into the void, his mind as large and empty as the sky above the Tonto Wilderness. He was simply at that spot, at that moment, with no further goal to pursue. There was nothing to do except sit. Whatever he had been before, whoever he would become, now he was just a man sitting on a cliff.

After several minutes, he understood this was what he had thanked Branson for: for bringing him to this moment. He might find his son; he might not. He might accomplish more in the world, receive more acclaim, or not. He could go back to his life in Philadelphia, or die alone in the woods. It didn't matter. It was all the same. He was on the Rim, and he was at peace.

He turned his eyes back toward the ponderosa forest, solid as a wall, where he'd wandered for three days. A pencil-thin shaft of sunlight caught a spot of blue, bright blue. Leaving his pack at the cliff, he walked toward it, expecting it to disappear when the trees moved in the next breeze; but it stayed as he entered the forest, and stayed as he approached the clearing.

He recoiled from the burned backhoe as if it were a rotting corpse. The wires were sprung, the steel twisted, the bucket flopped like the head of an agonized dinosaur. The bright Ellis blue was visible only where the flames had missed.

There was no rust; this had happened recently.

He felt like a soldier's parent, visiting the foreign battlefield where his son had died. That model was the pride of the Ellis fleet. Its safety record set the standard for the industry. Not one had ever been returned to the plant.

So what had happened to it?

On the fender was a carefully drawn human hand, scratched into the soot like a petroglyph on a cave wall, with a piece of turquoise in the palm.

He marked the location on his map. Following the narrow path the backhoe had torn through the trees, he wandered along the upper level of the Rim for a few miles, before dropping down to pick up his trail of surveyor's ribbons.

The lightness and peace he'd felt on the cliff evaporated, replaced by confusion. Geoffrey Ellis stumbled through the forest. After three days of wandering, all he'd found was a roasted backhoe.

Until he saw the Volvo. He must have passed it on his way out, without seeing it. It was huddled behind a huge rock.

Pennsylvania plates. Unlocked doors. In the back seat were some milkshake cups, water bottles, and a basketball. In the cargo area, a small pink bicycle.

Chapter 20

When Leah dipped her canteen under the trickle of water, she saw a sheet of ice ringing the edge of the tiny pool.

BJ couldn't work; Juana would not. She and Alissa played "hangman," drawing with a stick in the dust, keeping score with pebbles.

Leah sat outside her tent and pulled her whistle from her pocket. It was just a hollow bone, small and stained. But maybe it had worked with the fish. And Jim had played it the night when Juana axed herself. Perhaps those times it really had brought magic. She began to tootle idly, then with more purpose.

BJ's rumpled curls poked through the tent door.

"Medicine woman heap good flutist," she grinned. "Or is it flautist?"

Leah brought her tea. "Room service."

"I'm feeling better."

"Branson had words with Jim."

"Hoo, boy."

"Maybe more than words. They didn't look too friendly afterwards."

"Thanks, Leah."

"Thanks for?"

"Oh, make a list. Thanks for everything on it." BJ set her cup down. "Thanks for sending Branson out on his white horse."

"Rest. Heal."

BJ snuggled into the sleeping bags, her head out the tent flap, resting on Leah's knee. "So, I wanted to tell you something. Wanted to tell you I've learned my lesson. No more interesting men for me. No, siree, I'll take a boring guy any day."

"Bit late for that, don't you think?"

Tears oozed out of BJ's eyes and rolled off her cheeks. She wiped her nose and tried to laugh. "Got tears in my ears," she said.

❖ ❖ ❖ ❖ ❖

The next afternoon Leah knelt at the spring, waiting for water to trickle into the gourd. She was tired, burdened by living without hope.

She heard a footstep. Geoffrey stood beside her.

His face was twisted and streaked. He leapt across the stream and threw himself upon her, knocking her to the ground and burying his grubby head in her chest.

"Yesterday," he sobbed.

"Geoffrey, what?"

"Dad."

Leah's skin turned to rubber; her stomach rose to her mouth. The trees, rocks, sky, spun. She clutched Geoffrey, who lay like a corpse, and sat rocking him on the forest floor.

"Dad, he—"

"I understand. You don't have to say it."

Her body was a bag of sawdust. She screamed, she rocked, she hugged her son, but her body was sawdust. This was the moment she had dreaded, not knowing which of her beloveds she would lose first, but knowing that the day would come as sure as the sun would rise.

Geoffrey sat up and wiped his face on his sleeve. His freckles were almost invisible beneath the dirt and tears. "It was—Jim said wait there, he and Dad were going up the side to scout, but I got tired of waiting, and, and…"

"Shh, don't talk, you don't have to talk."

They sat, staring at the stream, at the overturned gourds, at their sneakered feet in the carpet of pine needles. Her body was numb; her mind floated high above the cliffs.

"Kaibito." Jim stepped out of the piñon behind them.

Leah didn't look up.

"You've told your mother. Now leave her alone to grieve."

"She needs me here."

Even through her numbness, Leah realized that was the first time she'd ever heard Geoffrey contradict Jim. He seemed to be a man talking, not her silent, obedient son.

Howlin' Jim stood at some distance and watched them sit by the stream. He said nothing as Leah and Geoffrey cried and hugged and wiped each other's faces with their sleeves.

"I'll be okay now," Leah said.

Geoffrey stood. Jim waited while the boy gathered his quiver and medicine bundle.

"Geoffrey, please stay."

"I'll come back soon."

"Let him go. He needs to be alone now." Jim watched as Geoffrey stumbled off into the forest.

Jim's face was painted white, the color of mourning. Though the air was frigid, he wore no shirt. His chest was painted in red circles and stars. He carried two rabbits on a string.

He handed her Branson's bundle. "Here. It's his medicine."

She looked at the bundle, at its strings and wraps, its feathers. She opened it and studied Branson's most precious things: his whistle, bags of powders, a trio of hollowed deer hooves tied with sinew. This bundle was the final measure of her man, heir to the Ellis Equipment fortune, admirer of the ancients, father of two. A bag of primitive superstitions.

Jim squatted beside her. "It's yours now."

"Tell me what happened."

"Leah."

"Don't touch me."

"Branson was my friend."

"I don't care what he was to you. Now tell me, so I can explain to Alissa, goddamn it."

Jim stared into the dark woods. "He got too close to the edge. He spotted a deer below and stepped out to take aim. It was a misstep."

"That's all."

"Yes."

"He died hunting."

"Yes. Bringing food for you. His neck was broken. He was dead when we got to him."

"What did Geoffrey do?"

"Kaibito understands. It's the way of nature. Nature doesn't play favorites. It kills without discrimination."

Leah stood up and hugged herself. The woods reeled around her. The world was crazy. She was crazy. Branson was dead, and she was crazy.

"We buried him. When you're ready, we'll take you there."

"Get away from me."

"I'll stay with you as long as you need me to."

She saw only a black pool, and a skinny, insane man standing before her. She felt only dizzy. She wished to have no feeling, ever.

"I'll care for you, Leah," Jim was saying. She heard his soft voice beyond the roar of blood that pulsed through her body, forcing her to live despite her ardent wish to be dead. "I'll protect you," she heard him say. "I'll hunt for you."

"Get away," she snarled.

She hit him on the chest, on the chin, seeing the white paint smear her knuckles as he stood erect, refusing to dodge or stop her fists. Only when she picked up a long branch and swung it at him did he melt into the woods.

Branson's death buried the camp like an avalanche. After the initial shrieks and tears, BJ and Juana went to their tent and refused to come out. Alissa lay in the sleeping bag with her mother and cried until she fell asleep.

The following afternoon, the little girl crawled out. Leah lifted the flap and watched her walk to the fire ring. Alissa gathered a few twigs and got a flame going. Her sneakers were full of holes, and she shivered in her thin jacket.

Leah was surprised to see Geoffrey join his sister. Having been unconscious for twenty-four hours, Leah didn't even know where her son had been, when he needed her so much.

He hugged Alissa, and they sat to warm their hands. Leah could see them talking. That was good; they should talk. The kids might have a future to talk about. She was going to spend the rest of her life, short though it might be, lying in the tent.

Jim, still painted white, came to the fire. He spoke to Geoffrey, and Geoffrey slouched off. Jim sat at the fire until Alissa wandered away to talk to her bent-twig doll near the partially built pithouse.

Leah lay in the sleeping bag, aware of Branson's presence in the close air. She felt no hunger or thirst, no cold, no need to talk.

BJ and Juana arrived at the fire circle. Jim brought rabbits and birds out of his bag and cooked them, though it was still daylight. Leah watched them eat. Alissa wouldn't come near the fire; Geoffrey hadn't returned.

Leah awoke after sunset to find Alissa sleeping next to her. Geoffrey and Juana sat at the fire. Jim gave BJ instructions, and she went to fetch her sleeping bag, to join him somewhere in the dark. Leah sat in her tent and watched Juana and Geoffrey until the fire went out.

Jim and Geoffrey still had to hunt. They left before daylight and returned with a young deer dangling over Jim's shoulders.

The tribe ate itself into a stupor. Jim praised Geoffrey's hunting ability. He said when the boy started his own tribe, he'd be a good leader, because he knew how to follow.

Geoffrey stared at the fire. Jim said nothing about Branson.

Three days later, they made the long pilgrimage to Branson's grave.

Jim and Geoffrey had laid him at the foot of a talus and piled rocks over him. Although Geoffrey now owned his father's arrows, they had left Branson's bow and quiver on the stones, the feathers fluttering in the cold wind. By spring the quiver would be mostly gone, carried off in pieces by birds and squirrels, converted to other uses by the animals of the Mogollon Rim. With freezes and thaws, more stones would tumble down, adding to and eventually obliterating the monument.

BJ and Juana couldn't stop crying. Leah shivered by the grave, longing to burrow beneath the stones, to see him, touch him, lie down beside him.

Howlin' Jim, no longer painted white, took a position by the grave and waited until everyone was quiet.

"Branson loved the ancients," he said. "Now they've welcomed him to them."

It sounded as if his speech was over; but he added, "When a tribe loses one of its hunters, the others have to manage without him. Young men sometimes have to take up their fathers' duties before they're ready." He looked at Leah. "Mothers have to release their sons. They have to let them be men."

He pulled out a prayer stick similar to the one he'd given Leah and laid it beside the quiver.

After a long silence, BJ stepped forward. Since Branson's death she had been working on a small figure of a deer. She had sculpted it with twigs and adobe, wrapped it in deerhide, and tied it with sinew. She laid it on the grave. "Goodbye, dear friend," she said.

Geoffrey put down his best obsidian point, the one that had killed his first deer. Alissa added a length of seeds she had strung into a necklace. Leah, still numb, hadn't thought to bring anything.

Juana stepped to the grave and spread Branson's old jacket over it. "Here," she said. "Thanks for letting me wear this. Thanks for getting all the food."

Howlin' Jim said, "Don't waste a good jacket, Juana."

"It's his."

He picked it up and shoved it at her. "Leave him something else. We'll need this."

"I want him to have it." Juana was crying.

"Don't be stupid."

"Up yours, Jim," she sobbed.

He kept his voice even. "You bray like a donkey every time I correct you. You don't do your duties, you don't build shelter. You waste your time and use foul language and throw away valuable items. You're afraid of everything." He shook her by the shoulders. "You are worthless."

Leah lunged at Jim, pounding him on the back. "Stop it! Leave her alone!"

He gave Juana a final shake and pushed her down. She sat on the rocks, clutching the jacket.

BJ wailed. Alissa sat on the rock pile, her whole body sobbing. BJ, Geoffrey, and Leah all held Juana, but the girl would not be comforted. Jim retreated to wait.

The weak light was fading, and the wind had picked up, already beginning to scatter their offerings. They had to get back to camp before night. Leah asked the others to start walking, saying she would catch up.

Jim shook his head. "I can't allow it. You could get lost, or do something foolish."

"Then leave Geoffrey with me."

"We'll all return together."

He and the others waited while she said goodbye to Branson. She still felt like sawdust. She sat on the grave and felt the wind blow away her tears before they rolled off her cheek.

But for all that blew into the wind, there would always be more tears.

Chapter 21

In the miserable camp the tents drooped like frozen flowers. Juana's tiny single tent leaned, its ties slack on one side, pegs pulling out of the rocky ground on the other. The few stones the women had gathered lay against the unimpressive ancient walls, becoming part of the ruin before they were even set into place.

Only the fire circle was alive. There were sitting logs, a chopping block, a wood supply, rocks and logs for countertops. Leah had found no burial at this site, no cache, nothing to indicate permanence. The camp must have sprung up from the ancients' necessity, like a cheap motel on a desert highway.

She saw BJ winding through the piñon, lugging two gourds and an armload of sticks, squinting in the morning sun. She'd spent the night in her hiding place and looked awful.

Leah ran to meet her. "Here, give me that. You shouldn't be lifting yet."

BJ sat by the fire. "Losing my sense of humor, Leah."

"Welcome to the club."

"Good news is, Jim hasn't found my cave."

"He hasn't looked."

"Even better."

Alissa coaxed Juana out of her tent. At the fire, she combed the big girl's hair and took a warm rag to her filthy face, as if she were the child. Juana seemed not to notice.

"Okay, troops," Leah said, trying to rally some energy. "Today we're going to set some new snares. Ready?"

BJ and Alissa were always ready, with their knives and game bags and drinking water.

"Juana?

"Nope."

"Aw, come on. You don't want to be here by yourself."

"Whatever."

"You don't like being alone."

Juana didn't answer. Leah was through arguing with her.

They set traps, extracted piñon nuts from cones, de-spined cactus, cracked walnuts. Nothing gave up without a fight.

Leah took little note of her new territory, since she'd lost interest in escaping. Why should she escape, leaving Branson under a pile of rocks? All she knew was that there was no easy water source at the new camp, and no natural shelter. The land was more open, but it was endless. Were they on top of the Rim, below it, beside it? What difference did it make?

So she rarely even checked her bearings. She glued her eyes to the ground, as an ancient would do, looking for food, with no plans beyond the hour she was living. BJ and Alissa led her back to camp.

Alissa scampered ahead, so she was the first to see.

"Mom?" She stood, frozen.

Juana lay next to the chopping block, right where they left her that morning. Her cup of tea waited on the grill. Except for the hatchet in her hand, nothing had been moved. Except for the quarreling magpies surrounding her, no one was there.

Blood had long since stopped spurting from her wrist. She lay on the brown-stained earth, eyes closed. Her jacket of rabbit skins was caked and clotted.

BJ screamed. She screamed again. Leah didn't try to stop her. She sat on the log and cradled Alissa, rocking, rocking. Numbness had become her natural state.

She felt tired, and terribly, terribly guilty.

Jim painted himself to the waist and went shirtless in the cold day as he dug the grave.

Leah, BJ, and Alissa washed Juana's body, soaking the hardened blood in pot after pot of warm water, scrubbing the face, the fingers, the hair, dumping the red liquid far from camp to keep away animals. They welcomed the sense of purpose their activity gave them.

Alissa braided Juana's hair and strung a crown of pinecones. BJ washed the rabbit skin jacket and fastened it around Juana with a toggle she carved from deer antler. She wrapped a soft bracelet of fur around the mangled wrist. Leah wove a mat of yucca, and each of them held a corner to carry Juana to the grave.

After the last stone was set, they sat beside it. Nobody talked, not even Howlin' Jim. They stared into the piñon and pine woods.

At least it wasn't snowing.

Days passed while Leah floated on a raft of sorrow and guilt. She didn't notice Howlin' Jim and Geoffrey leaving to hunt each morning, returning to sit by the fire in the evenings. She didn't see BJ slip away to the woods when the men arrived in camp. She didn't notice there was game to clean, wood to gather, a ragged child wandering about camp, as oblivious as she was.

One day she became aware that Jim still applied white paint each morning. Why did he paint for Juana, whom he scorned, when he had painted only once for Branson?

He made no overtures toward her. He sat by himself and spoke only to Geoffrey.

One morning she followed him out of camp, knowing he knew she was there. He knelt beside a rock that served as a table and stirred a bit of chalky substance into a tiny bowl of grease. Studying his face in his sliver of mirror, he prepared to repaint. Leah saw him dab his eyes. He had to go over his cheeks several times.

He was crying. Crying like an ordinary, brokenhearted man. Leah's numbness turned to mild surprise.

When he finished, he wiped out the bowl, tied the bag of powder, and stood to face her. His stern expression was back in place, softened only a bit by the fresh layer of white.

"What do you want?"

"Why do you still paint?"

"I'll paint as long as I mourn. I may paint until my own death."

"Why do you mourn for Juana?"

"I don't only mourn for Juana. She's just one component of my greater loss. I'm mourning the death of promise."

"I don't understand."

"We had a fine vision."

"You did. I didn't."

"My mistake. Now we have no prospect for survival as a tribe. Branson failed us. Juana and Kaibito offered hope, but Juana also failed us. Our last chance is gone." He turned to leave.

"Jim, please."

His stare was cold. Leah had no power, she was his prisoner, and he no longer respected her.

"You're going to beg me to take you back."

"Yes."

"As if that erroneous civilization could satisfy you now."

"As if I might be alive on my next birthday."

"Pleading doesn't become you. You squandered your powers. Now you're groveling."

"Yes, I am."

He stared at nothing, barely breathing. "You've won," he said. "I concede."

Leah blinked several times. "What have I won?"

When he looked at her again, she saw a man who might have died hundreds of years before. He looked like a petroglyph, a man with no features.

"You got what you wanted."

"What I wanted?"

"We've become a nuclear family, as you wanted. We're not a tribe. You have your children, and I'm your provider. You've taken us back to what we left behind. You've made me into exactly what I didn't want to be."

"I can't believe what I'm hearing."

"You used your power to destroy our tribe. We have no choice now, except to live with what you created."

"I didn't do this."

"Leave me. I don't want to see you."

Geoffrey Ellis dashed up the cement walk to Vern's house. Mrs. Crouse put him on the sofa and brought him a glass of water.

"There, now, Jeff."

"I've been hyperventilating for two days. Sorry to come into your clean house all dirty like this."

"That's how it is, camping."

Vern entered through the kitchen door, preceded by his stomach. "Hey, woodsman, I've missed you. Done nothing except eat since you left. Wow, you look like you ran a marathon."

"I found their car."

"Whoa, no kidding."

"I have to go back up there."

"I'll call the sheriff. We can leave in the morning."

Geoffrey Ellis hadn't considered this. "I don't want the sheriff. We'll find them ourselves."

The cushions let out a wheeze as Vern sat beside him. "Listen, Jeff, up till now this was just a hunch. Now that you've found the car, we're talking about a possible crime."

"Vern, my son's strange, but he's not a criminal."

"You and I know that, but an abandoned car in the woods looks suspicious. There was a girl missing from the high school, several weeks back. They had volunteer searchers, sniffer dogs, para-psychologists, the whole bit. People are still freaked out."

"Why fuel the flame, then?" Geoffrey Ellis decided not to mention the backhoe, at least not yet.

Vern looked at his wife.

She said, "Jeff, we know who you are. "

Geoffrey Ellis put his head in his hands. "I'm sorry I didn't tell you."

Vern patted him on the shoulder. "It wasn't hard to figure out."

"For most people, it puts a different perspective on their dealings with me. I wanted to avoid that."

"We understand.

"And I'm trying to keep the press out of this."

"Of course. We haven't said a word."

"So, will you go up with me?"

"This kinda puts me in a tight spot, Jeff. You know this is Thanksgiving week? There'll be hunters needing me here."

"Oh, Vern," said Mrs. Crouse, "I'll manage the station for you."

"You shouldn't have to be stuck with that."

"It wouldn't be the first time. Go on, Vern, Jeff needs you more than a bunch of drunk hunters. I wish they'd all stay home anyway."

Vern sat staring at his wife until Geoffrey Ellis stood up. "Guess I'll go by myself, then." With a little bow, he handed Mrs. Crouse his water glass and stepped toward the door. "I want you to know I appreciate everything you've done. Now, if you'll excuse me, I have to re-stock my food supply."

Vern sighed. "How am I supposed to argue with the CEO of a major American corporation and my wife, both?"

Geoffrey Ellis grinned. "You're not, Vern. Thank you."

Mrs. Crouse saw him to the door. "Just be back Thursday for Thanksgiving dinner."

They left at dawn. Geoffrey Ellis was sore in every part of his body, but he slapped his hands together and stamped his feet for warmth as he loaded the SUV at the motel. Anyone awake at that hour would see a trim gray-haired man, moving with more purpose than most forty-year-olds, flinging his pack and tent through the hatch of the car, as if he'd spent a lifetime starting before dawn—which, of course, he had.

He felt alive. A hot meal, a long shower, and a night on a mattress had recharged him. Besides, he wasn't alone anymore. He had a friend with him.

Vern dozed as they drove up the face of the Rim among the trees that stood frosted, waiting for sunrise. His wife's sandwiches were scrunched into his backpack. She had also sent along a stew, frozen in plastic bags, for their first night out; after that, their meals would be freeze-dried. Vern hoped they'd find what they were looking for soon. The measure of a twenty-first-century wilderness man was how many days he could live on freeze-dried. Vern wasn't interested in setting any records.

Geoffrey Ellis had studied the map. There was a short cut to the dotted-line road he'd taken his first time out. He turned onto the Forest Service access, hoping the bump and shake would wake Vern so he'd have some company. It didn't. Not until he left the clay surface and began maneuvering around stumps and rocks did Vern stretch his arms and open his eyes.

"That's right," he said. "Go on in there. Doesn't look like you can get through, but you can."

"You know this path."

"Uh huh." Vern crossed his arms and dropped his chin back onto his chest.

The sun was well up when Geoffrey Ellis stopped the car. If he took it any farther, they'd never get it out.

Groaning under heavy packs, they walked a few hundred feet into the forest. Geoffrey Ellis felt as though he were carrying a building on his back. He spotted one of the fluorescent ribbons he'd left tied to a branch.

Vern puffed ahead of him. "Now, what idiot would leave his ribbons tied to the trees?"

"This idiot. Those are my ribbons."

Vern grinned. "Oh, hey, good thinking, Jeff. Shows a lot of foresight, marking your path like that."

They slapped each other companionably on the backpacks and started out.

Chapter 22

Leah squatted by the tiny spring, struggling to fill the gourds. Geoffrey stepped out of the woods.

"Mom."

"Where's Jim?"

"He's right behind me. Quick, Mom, listen."

"You're back early."

"Mom. Jim killed Dad."

Leah dropped the gourd and stared at Geoffrey. His face was twisted into a grimace.

"I saw him do it. He doesn't know. He thinks I was waiting below. He pushed Dad over."

Leah, still not registering what she'd heard, said, "Oh," and went back to filling her gourds.

Geoffrey shook her by the shoulders. "Mom, did you hear me?" He stopped and listened. "Here he comes. Walk in front of me."

Leah felt as if she was just waking up. She grabbed the half-filled gourds and loped up the hill. Jim must not see her face. She gasped for breath, feeling there wasn't enough oxygen in the air to keep her heart beating. She heard Geoffrey's soft footsteps behind her. A murderer was padding along directly behind her son.

She strode through camp, dropping the gourds at the wall.

"Mom?" Alissa started to follow, carrying her twig doll.

"Not now."

She brushed past the girl, crawled into her tent, and buried her head under the sleeping bag. She had to scream, but didn't dare. She couldn't talk to Geoffrey. She couldn't look at Jim. She could do nothing.

Except refuse to breathe. She held her breath until her chest was ready to explode. Her head thumped, her chapped cheeks tingled, and still she would not breathe. Lights spun around her head like fireflies, until she fainted.

When she came to, she was breathing normally. She couldn't even stop the pain by suffocating herself.

❖   ❖   ❖   ❖   ❖

If he saw her face, he would know she knew. She didn't go to the fire that evening. Alissa brought her food, but Leah's throat was so knotted she couldn't talk or eat. She just held her daughter, the meat growing cold.

In the morning Geoffrey and Jim were gone. If Geoffrey stayed quiet about Branson, would Jim keep him as a son, a partner? How long could Geoffrey stay quiet?

How long could she? For two days she gagged on the words. At night she held them down, with a hand on her throat. If she were to speak, she would say them, and that would be the end of them all.

She had to stay away from BJ and Alissa.

BJ tried to hug her once. "Leah, it's me," she whispered into Leah's plastered tangle of hair. "Cry on me. Talk to me."

Leah pushed her off. After that, BJ and Alissa left her alone.

In her tent, or wandering through the piñon, Leah imagined Branson's death. She saw his argument with Jim that morning after BJ crawled into their tent. Perhaps Branson threatened him. Perhaps the men raised their voices or shoved each other. Maybe that was the moment Jim decided to eliminate him. She remembered the doom she felt when they left camp. She saw them head toward the cliffs where they could spot game browsing below.

She saw Branson poised on the ledge. His hair was tied back, and his jeans, too baggy for his lank frame, were kept up with a strip of tanned hide. His lean arm held the bow; his other hand was ready to snatch an arrow from his quiver and fit it onto the string. Howlin' Jim crouched nearby. She saw her son, below the cliff, disobey Jim and climb up to join them. Branson waited until the deer wandered into a clearing, then stepped forward and took aim. As he pulled the string, Jim lunged.

Leah saw Geoffrey stuff his fist into his mouth and race to the bottom, where he had to wait for Jim to bring him the news. He had to hear Jim tell him what he already knew, listen to Jim lie, and he had to react like a man—

not with screams, but with silent acceptance. And he had to bury his father under a pile of rocks.

For two days she watched the story unfold in her head. Over and over she rewrote it, with herself scripted in, drawing an arrow of her own and sending it through Howlin' Jim's skinny chest. In another version she saw her ancient hunter emerge from his burial cavern and plunge a bone knife through Jim's neck. As Jim died at her feet, the ancient nodded to her and disappeared.

Leah walked around as Branson used to do, listening to the forest and to voices no one else could hear, unaware of her daughter and BJ following her.

On the third morning she heard her own voice say, "BJ. Alissa."

They dashed over and threw their arms around her.

"I thought you'd never talk again!" BJ cried. "I thought you'd never talk!"

"I'm okay."

"You're okay! You're talking!"

Leah studied their faces, seeing them for the first time in days, remembering she had loved them in another time and place. BJ had cut Alissa's bangs, so that her eyes shone like the glass eyes of a charming, abandoned doll. BJ looked like a homeless woman Leah remembered in Philadelphia, with layers of ill-fitting clothes incapable of warming her skeletal body.

She smiled at them. "I have to go to the woods now."

"Don't go. Stay here and talk with us."

Alissa clung to her. "Take me, Mom!"

"I have to go alone."

"I want to go with you! Every time Howlin' Jim comes back to camp, BJ goes away. What if she leaves me?"

BJ was ashamed. "I never go for long, Liss. And I don't leave, unless Geoffrey's here with you. Have I ever?"

"No. But I want you to take me with you."

"Okay, twerp. If I go, you'll go with me."

"Promise."

"I promise."

Leah said, "You hide, Alissa hides with you."

"I hide, she hides."

Leah pried Alissa off and wandered into the forest.

Snow had fallen during the night, and patches remained in the shadows. The air was cold. Bundled in every item of her own clothing, a sweatshirt of Branson's, and her wool hat and gloves, she stumbled down to an over-hang that she considered to be hers. Here she sat, as still as the rock itself.

This was how her life would end, then: in the cold woods, with no protection from the reality that nature's other creatures understood by instinct.

She'd never get any magic. She'd never get the strength to combat Jim. She would drift away from her children. Her dreams, her past would float away. One day she would walk into the woods and not return. She would die of starvation, exposure, a broken heart. Her body would lie on the forest floor, to be consumed by scavengers. First, coyotes would drag her bones away, and then magpies would clean their leavings. Then the ants, and finally microorganisms, until no recognizable part of her would exist.

The thought was comforting. Perhaps she was letting go. Perhaps she had to accept death to find her magic, as Jim had said. Or perhaps Jim was full of it, as Juana had said.

Whatever was going to happen, she didn't care. She leaned back, humming to herself the way Alissa did, and let the rock's indifference cradle her.

"Mom."

Geoffrey stepped from behind the rock. He was stooped and panting under Branson's huge expedition pack. He wasn't wearing his necklace of bones and fetishes.

"Why aren't you with Jim?"

"We split up to hunt. I got away. He won't miss me for a couple of hours."

"Oh." Leah had never been so lacking in curiosity.

"We've got to go. I brought food and extra clothes."

"Go where?"

"The old camp. He won't look there. He'll think I took the east route." Leah was suddenly alert. "What east route?"

"Dad knows it—knew it. They told me about it. It's the shortest way to the top of the Rim. Our old camp's a long way in the opposite direction, but after we get there, I know the shortcut out."

Leah jumped up. Geoffrey knew about the crack in the bowl. He knew the way out. "I'll get Alissa and BJ."

"Mom, no. They can't move fast enough. We've got to put several miles behind us before he figures out we're gone."

"I won't leave them."

"If they came, we'd be as easy to track as a herd of buffalo. We have to go alone."

"I won't leave them with him. He might, he could—"

"He won't hurt them. He's not afraid of them. Mom, either you come with me or I go by myself."

"No!"

"If I do get out alone, he'll make the rest of you move again, and I'll never find you."

"Then stay, Geoffrey. You can't leave us."

"He'll know something's up soon. He'll get back to camp and see Dad's pack is gone."

"Oh, my god, what have you done?"

"He'll start searching the east route. That'll give us a head start."

Leah stared at him. All the time she had been mourning and listless, he was planning, strategizing, gathering supplies. He was as cunning as Jim. His face was set, his eyes fixed.

"If he catches me now, he'll kill me."

So it was that simple.

Leah let him load her up with provisions, though he kept most of the weight in his father's pack. Her body and brain were awakening from the twilight of anguish. Her feet, filled with lead, took a step away from camp, then another and another.

They walked for an hour. She stopped to look back at the wall of trees. Even if she turned back now, she'd never find camp.

She'd made her choice. A choice that had a minuscule possibility of survival, over one that assured death for all.

Without warning, her legs crumpled. She lay on the soft carpet of pine needles, hugging her knees, bawling into the shredded denim of her jeans.

"I'm sorry, Alissa," she sobbed. "I'm sorry, BJ. Goodbye, goodbye, I'm so sorry."

They trudged for hours. Geoffrey changed directions often, but he moved with confidence. Whenever possible he led her over outcrops, to leave no sign, and picked the most illogical paths—choosing difficult stream crossings, slipping through tight spots. Leah wondered if his precautions would do any good; after all, he'd learned them from Jim.

At mid-afternoon, with many miles behind them, they stopped to eat some dried meat. Everything looked the same, nothing looked familiar. By dusk they were in an area of dense underbrush, difficult to move through.

Geoffrey turned Leah's flashlight on long enough to heap branches for a bed, and was asleep the moment he lay down.

Leah heard the gurgle of water. A thin rivulet trickled beneath the brambles. She filled their bottles.

The bushes had berries. Though desiccated, they offered the promise of a bite of sweet. She gathered some in the dark and put them to her lips.

The scent was distinctive. They were western soapberries.

Fighting sleep, she set to work. There was the stream to enlarge, a pool to create under the overhang of brush. She scooped and scraped and built up the lower rim with mud and branches, as a beaver would build a dam, until she had made a small bowl with a good exchange of water.

Then she blew into her whistle. The sound was high and breathy, barely audible—but it was for the trout, not Jim, to hear. Though she was numb with exhaustion, she felt alive again. Even with the odds against her, at least she was doing something for their survival. The ancients would approve. She blew the whistle until her eyes closed.

They awoke to a gray dawn, wrapped in a cocoon of cold. Their jackets were coated with frost, toes and fingers dead.

A trout floated belly-up in the tiny pool. They gobbled the icy flesh and licked the oil off their fingers, then buried the bones and reconstructed the brambles to look undisturbed.

By the middle of the day, the territory was familiar. Leah had been here. Their steps quickened. In late afternoon, they reached their old spring.

"It feels like home," Leah said.

"It was home. Dad was here with us."

They filled their bottles, trudged up the hill, and collapsed in the cave, against the walls of the buildings the women had built. Coming upon it fresh, Leah thought the rooms looked like authentic Mogollon ruins. But she remembered every stone, every smudge of plaster mixed with the blood of her scraped fingers.

Geoffrey dumped the heavy pack. They snuggled against the walls, basking in the reflected warmth the autumn sun. By now, Jim would have figured it out. He would have questioned BJ and Alissa.

And where would he find them? Would they be in the woods, gathering berries and setting snares? Would he surprise them at camp while they worked on their sewing? Maybe Chaco arrived in camp before Jim, giving BJ enough warning to rush Alissa to her hiding place. But of course, Jim would find them.

Leah rolled in remorse, seeing him confront the confused BJ. Picturing Alissa, at the moment she learned her mother and brother were gone. But every minute Jim spent with them bought her and Geoffrey another minute to run.

Jim would head for the east route. He would soon find a cold trail, no confirming clues; and then he'd turn around and come this way. And he would not be in any mood to talk.

But they had to rest.

"We need a fire, Geoffrey. I'm cold and starving."

"We don't have anything to cook. It's too risky, anyway."

"He could be miles away."

"Or not. I think he'd head straight for the shortcut, to catch us at the exit. But if we build a fire, he might smell the smoke."

"You're right."

Geoffrey sat up. "Tell you what. I'll go check some of the old snares. If there's anything edible, we'll risk a small fire."

She smiled at him. "Deal. Be careful."

He slipped over the edge of the cliff and disappeared.

Vern Crouse and Geoffrey Ellis puffed through the ponderosa near the edge of the Rim, following the trail of fluorescent ribbons. Though his pack was as heavy as before, Geoffrey Ellis hardly noticed. Vern's company made the trek easier.

I'm almost happy, he thought, when he thought at all. He didn't understand, but he wasn't surprised.

By mid afternoon they arrived at the Volvo. Geoffrey Ellis stood back while Vern inspected it. He had prepared himself; he'd had time to process the basketball, the pink bike, time to picture his son and daughter-in-law bumping through the forest on that front seat.

Geoffrey Ellis noted that Vern didn't touch. "You've done this sort of thing before."

"I'm afraid I have. But this one sure doesn't broadcast clues. Coercion, foul play, none of that. Looks like an organized exit."

"Consenting parties, you mean?"

"Yeah."

"You ready to walk some more? I have something else to show you."

They walked until they spotted the twisted hulk of the backhoe, silhouetted against the sunset.

"Good lord," said Vern.

"So why would this thing be out here, hours from a road?"

"Looks like pot hunters," Vern sighed. "I thought those days were over. Besides, there aren't any ruins near here." He struggled out of his pack and sat heavily on it. "It's a mystery."

"And why's it burned? Who'd do that?"

"Maybe the engine blew up?"

"Ellis engines don't blow up. Here, take a look at this." Geoffrey Ellis shone his flashlight at the drawing of the hand.

"That's weird."

"I thought so."

"You see any possible connection with your son?"

"I'm thinking, well, no real thoughts. But it's too coincidental, the car and the backhoe only a couple miles apart."

The men camped near the machine. By lantern light, they studied their maps. The night was cold; a wind blew in, driving them into their tents early. Despite his discomfort and unanswered questions, Geoffrey Ellis fell asleep contented, and woke up not too stiff.

The next day they fanned through the woods between the car and the backhoe, leaving trails of ribbons. In one direction the forest seemed endless; in another, they kept running into unscalable cliffs. After three frustrating days, they knew they had to go back in the morning.

Geoffrey Ellis, his heart heavier now, agreed to let Vern notify the sheriff. Branson and Leah and the kids were dead. All he could hope was to learn what happened. He rolled up his sleeping bag and took down his tent, stopping from time to time to listen to the woods, as if the trees might yet have something to tell him. Then he began the long trudge back to the edge of the Rim.

They reached the SUV by late afternoon. Geoffrey Ellis opened the tailgate and used it to hold his pack while he extricated his arms. Vern took a long swig of water and wiped his face with a handkerchief.

"I'm sorry, Jeff."

"Our best shot wasn't good enough."

"Yeah. After the holiday we'll get a search party going. It'll be more efficient."

Geoffrey Ellis sat on the tailgate, staring into the forest. "Search and rescue, that's what they call it, I guess."

"I'm afraid it'll be more search and recover. The chances of anyone being alive after this long…."

"I understand."

"But it might be of some comfort to find out what happened to them."

Geoffrey Ellis said, "You know what I'm thinking, Vern?"

"Can't say I do."

"I'm thinking maybe I haven't given it my best shot, after all. I'm thinking I ought to go back in."

Vern looked at him with sympathy. "I know how you feel. But you've done everything you could, figuring it out, finding the evidence. Now it's time to get help."

Geoffrey Ellis stood up and began digging through his pack. "I've got another day's food and water here in the car." He pulled out his trash and emptied the pack of everything but the essentials. Over Vern's protests, he re-stocked it with jerky and energy bars, refilled his water bottles, and put the pack back on. "I swear, I think it's heavier than it was before."

"Hey, Jeff, really, I got to insist now."

Geoffrey Ellis fumbled in his pocket. "Here's the car key. Give me one more day."

"Hey, no."

"One more day." He walked toward the forest, turned and waved. "Thanks, Vern."

Chapter 23

Geoffrey was gone a long time. Leah had to stop worrying about him. She had to stop thinking about scared little Alissa, about her own guilt, about Branson lying broken under a pile of rocks, about Juana, whose only escape was to pour out her blood. Leah had to stop cowering at every pop of a twig or groan of a ponderosa branch. She made herself turn off the picture of Howlin' Jim stalking them through the woods.

She walked around the outcrop to her burial cave.

"I'm back," she said. She tiptoed past the standing slabs, past the ancient who lay sleeping beneath her. Nothing had changed. The brambles still lay over the cache, a few dry leaves crackling and blowing against the cave wall.

She retrieved her bowl and fetish from their hiding place, then sat by the grave and licked her fingers to wipe out the bowl's matte-black interior. She breathed a few breaths through her whistle, and laid the whistle, her prayer twig, and Jim's turquoise nuggets into the bowl with the obsidian fetish: all her magic in one place.

The significance of the fat dark fetish, with its tiny beads, still puzzled her. She turned it over in her hand, rubbing the fulsome belly, laying her other hand on her own hollow one. Her bottom was bony; her clothes hung around her. But the fetish was plump.

Can it be that simple? she wondered. The ancients valued a full stomach. Maybe the fetish wasn't pregnant, but just well fed. Was that its message?

Of course. There's food in the burial chamber. I was in such a hurry to hide it, I forgot about those pots of beans and corn down there.

She leapt to her feet and began to paw the earth around the lowest standing slab, heedless of where the sand flew. She reached the prehistoric fabric, laid it aside, and disassembled the lattice of twigs. Rocks and dirt skittered down inside, enlarging the hole. She hauled up two slabs, wrestled them onto the ground, got her flashlight out of her pack, and aimed its beam inside.

The ancient skeleton still slept with his weapons and pots of grain. The ladder still leaned against the wall.

She eased into the opening, bracing her arms on either side, inching her toes down the sloping wall until they touched the top rung of the ladder. A step at a time, down, down she climbed, until she stood on the floor of the cavern. Dust swirled about her feet. She swept her flashlight beam around the walls.

There were more skeletons, five in all, carefully laid out, surrounded by pots and artifacts. Every skull was covered with a bowl; all arms were crossed, paper skin holding fragile bones together.

How did they die? Who lived to bury them?

Her ears pounded. But it wasn't ancient drums, just her own blood racing through her body, loud in the silence of the grave.

My woman; my bowl maker. She was the only member of the tribe left alive. And when she finally died, she was alone, like the rest of the forest creatures, with no one to bury her.

Spooked, and mourning for the ancients as well as her own people, she rushed to the nearest pot and thrust her hands in. She filled her pockets with corn and dust.

"Thank you," she whispered, and crawled back up the ladder into the sunlight.

She built a tiny fire of twigs and heated water in two metal cups. She poured the corn from hand to hand, blew the dust out of it, ground it between two rocks, and put it on to boil.

By the time Geoffrey returned with a small bird, the mush was simmering. Leah had started replacing the thatch of sticks across the enlarged hole, using longer branches to span the extra width.

"Don't say anything, Geoffrey. Yes, it's a burial. There are five skeletons down there. But it's okay. They left corn for us, to give us strength. Will you eat some?"

He nodded.

"Do you want to look in, before we cover it up?"

"I don't think so."

"Okay. Then help me with this."

They finished the latticework. With the extra length of the twigs, Leah feared it wouldn't support the weight of a sand-filled pot. They decided to lay the slabs across the opening rather than plant them upright in the earth. It wasn't historically correct, but it would be more stable.

"Corn's ready. We'll lift those slabs into place after we eat."

Leah buried the little fire. *I hope this is the last sunset I'll ever see from the Mogollon Rim,* she thought. The stars appeared quickly, bringing out the sounds of night. They each had one bite of bird breast and dipped their fingers into the hot, gritty mush.

"Good," said Geoffrey.

"You're as chatty as your father."

Geoffrey smiled. "While Dad was here, this made sense to me. But now it's just, it's—"

"Crazy?"

"Worse than crazy. I hate Howlin' Jim. I wish he was dead. I can't believe I thought he was cool."

"Your dad thought he was cool."

"Mom? We burned up somebody's backhoe."

"I know. I saw it."

"You did?"

"Yes."

"Then you were almost out. You could've gone out."

"If I'd left, I never would've found you guys again."

Geoffrey leaned against the cave wall and sighed. "Dad said he had to, like, get rid of Grandpa Geoffrey because he makes machines for criminals. But I wasn't sure. I felt like we were the criminals. I mean, we burned up this guy's backhoe. I never even met the person. I don't even know he was a criminal."

"You got sucked in."

"I'm sorry I did that."

"Look, Geoffrey, Dad and I were the parents. You were the kid. Parents are supposed to teach the kids what's right."

"I shouldn't have believed Jim."

"Dad shouldn't have either."

"I shouldn't have kept secrets from you."

"And I shouldn't have let them bring us out here in the first place. There are plenty of shouldn'ts for all of us."

"That stuff Dad said about killing his father, I believed him."

"Until he died, himself."

"Yeah."

Though the cave was dark, she knew he was crying. She gathered the boy to her, patted his near man-sized shoulders, and raked his grubby hair with her fingers.

"Geoffrey, it was Jim who killed your father. Not you."

❖　❖　❖　❖　❖

Geoffrey Ellis staggered under his backpack. Maybe it was a mistake to go back in. He and Vern had already looked everywhere. They'd combed the woods around the backhoe and car for two days. They kept running into that cliff, too steep to climb down and too wide to get around. There was nowhere else. And exhaustion was riding his shoulders, along with his backpack.

But here he was. Besides, Vern had the car.

He staggered along until the light was gone, following the ribbons he'd left, then took out his flashlight and kept going. Though only hours had passed, it seemed days before he reached the turnoff to the abandoned car. The ponderosa absorbed all light from the starry sky. His boots caught on rocks, and branches scratched his face as he felt his way from marker to marker.

In near total darkness, he stumbled toward the big rock. His flashlight picked out the glint of the Volvo's bumper, and he sat down. He was asleep before he even got out of his pack.

Hours later, he awoke. He blinked. He could see as much with his eyes closed as open. Where was the flashlight? He dragged his arm out of the strap of the backpack, felt the ground, patted a circle around himself with his hand.

Could I have dropped it? He blinked again, saw nothing. He heard an owl's hoot, the swoosh of wings. He heard a twig snap behind him.

"Hello?"

Another twig snapped. Geoffrey Ellis swerved around.

"Branson? Is that you?"

Again he heard the owl, then nothing.

"Branson, it's your father." He waited. "Leah?"

There was only the rustle of leaves. It could be the breeze; it could be a rabbit or a bird.

"Branson, please, let me know you're alive."

I may be talking to my son, or I may be talking to the wind.

"I understand now. You don't have to say a word. Just give me a sign. Just so I can know you're alive. I won't try to make you leave."

He stood, waiting. Another rustling of leaves.

A whack on the back of his head sent him staggering to his knees. He tried to take a step, but his legs gave out and he toppled into the brush. In his last moment of consciousness, he tasted the earth on his tongue. Finally, he could see the stars.

In the cave, Leah switched on her flashlight to make sure they had everything. She put the metal cups, her ancient bowl, and the fetish into her pack. Geoffrey strapped on Branson's big pack and climbed topside to determine which path to use to exit camp. The shortcut was so fast, he said, that they'd be on top of the Rim in a couple of hours. Leah couldn't imagine how, but she was learning to accept gifts, so she believed it.

All they had to do was lift the slabs over the hole, and leave. Leah shone her light down through the twig thatch, faintly illuminating the skull of her ancient hunter.

"Thank you," she whispered. "We'll go now."

She waited by the hole for Geoffrey, flicking the light around, painting the jagged sides of the cave in broad strokes.

The light caught a pair of eyes.

Chaco bounded into the cave.

Leah fell backward on the sand. Where Geoffrey had stood moments before, there stood a weedy figure, silhouetted against the night sky. His braid hung behind him, his buckskin leggings stirred in the breeze. He wore his quiver full of arrows.

"You called me."

"I didn't call you."

"You called me with your whistle and man-stick." He took a step into the cave.

"Stay there. Don't come any closer."

"Come with me."

"No!" She spoke very loud. Geoffrey must hear her.

"Your daughter needs you."

"I said don't move."

"You see? You're stronger now. You're not begging."

When she didn't reply, he said, "I'll teach you how to use that strength. I'll teach you to become powerful."

"I don't want your help!" she shouted, for Geoffrey. She knew Jim couldn't see her as well as she saw him, standing against the sky.

His voice was softer now, soothing. "What is there for you out there? Do you really believe you can return to that vacuous life?" He learned toward her, whispering. "And Leah, I want you. I want to guide your will."

She sat motionless. Even if he couldn't see her, he could hear her move, just as he could hear a rabbit in the brush.

"I'll teach you magic. You'll be my mate."

"The tribe is dead."

"Yes. I regret that. But there's still time for us."

She maneuvered a few inches. He didn't move, but he was listening, calculating the distance between them.

"You killed Branson."

His head turned toward her.

"You murdered him," she said.

"Branson violated the rules. He became soft in his thinking. His actions, and yours, brought down the tribe."

Jim shifted his weight. "I knew your husband better than you did. He said he had left his former life, but he held on to it. He tried to hide that from me. And he challenged me, but he was weak. That's why he died."

She began to inch away from the hole.

"You have nowhere to go." He took another step toward her. "I want you to come willingly." His voice was smooth as his gleaming muscles. "I'll give you time to mourn."

A large, ungainly figure stepped into the cave. Geoffrey, wearing Branson's big pack, stopped a few feet behind Jim. Chaco sniffed Geoffrey's leg and wagged his tail.

"Kaibito," said Jim, without turning.

"Leave him alone," Leah blurted. "Geoffrey, get away."

"Kaibito has inherited his father's willfulness, and his secrecy." Jim's voice was sharp. "But Kaibito is young, and I need him as a hunter."

Leah stood. "Geoffrey, go."

"Kaibito, don't be more foolish than your father, and your grandfather."

Leah heard something—perhaps fear, perhaps gloating—in Jim's voice. "What do you know about Geoffrey's grandfather?"

"That he's stubborn. Brave. Willing to venture beyond his capability."

"Why do you know that?"

Jim shifted. "And sentimental, to his own detriment. A man of that age, raised in civilization, has no chance of survival on the Rim. He'll learn that, if he lays eyes on your car again."

What was Jim saying? Leah had learned that silence has power. She waited.

"I looked for you at your car," Jim said. "But I found someone else instead."

Geoffrey spoke for the first time, his voice breaking. "You saw my grandfather?"

"I doubt he'll remember the encounter." Jim took another step toward Leah. "Enough talk. Kaibito, are you willing to work for another chance?"

Geoffrey inched closer.

"Don't push me, Kaibito."

"All right," Geoffrey mumbled.

"What did you say?"

"All right."

"Good. Now tell your mother to come with us. Last chance, Kaibito."

When Geoffrey still didn't speak, Jim said, "You force me to do this. First your mother, then you."

He stepped toward Leah. She held her breath, suddenly understanding what Geoffrey was doing. She saw the dog sniff at the ground outside the cave. She scooted farther back, putting the hole between herself and Jim.

"Okay, we'll go with you," she said. She saw Jim take a step toward her. "I said okay, don't hurt us."

Jim took another step.

Geoffrey lunged at Jim with the full weight of his body and the heavy pack. They both went down. Chaco disappeared.

Leah heard the crackle of breaking sticks, the thud of fists against skull, the scuff of deerskin in the sand. She heard feet struggling for a hold. She heard Geoffrey's breath forced out of his lungs as he fell beneath the backpack, and Jim's angry growl as he tried to get on top. But Geoffrey, using the pack, shoved him like a rock before the blade of a bulldozer.

Leah ran behind Jim and pushed. His hand grabbed her ankle, clawing her to the ground as his legs slipped over the edge of the cavern. She clasped a standing slab and held on, her shoulders straining against their sockets, as his arms winched her toward the dangling void. With her other foot she kicked and kicked, until her heel made contact with his forehead. His nails tore her skin as his hold on her leg loosened.

With a nauseating whump, a groan, a skitter of pebbles, Jim was at the bottom of the hole.

Leah backed against the wall of the cave and shrieked. Geoffrey hauled himself up, dumped off the pack, and began scooping up stones—small ones, large ones, some too heavy to lift—and hurling and shoving them into the cavern. Rocks, sticks, sand, anything he could put his hands around, crashed and clattered beneath them.

"Geoffrey! Stop!"

He slung one last handful of dirt and stood up, panting.

Leah scrambled around the cave until she found the flashlight. Hands trembling, she switched on the beam and aimed it into the hole.

When the whirlwind of dust settled, they saw that Jim's fall had knocked the ladder down. It lay at an angle across his splayed body. His arm was twisted behind him as if frozen in the act of pulling an arrow from his quiver. He was face to face with the sleeping ancient.

Chaco slunk into the cave, crawled on his belly to the hole, and hung his head down inside. Leah and Geoffrey leaned against the wall, watching stars move past the ponderosa in the brilliant, cold sky. The moon was rising. A fresh breeze scattered leaves around the cave.

Leah stuck the flashlight into a cranny, giving them enough light to move around. Without a word they each picked up an end of a stone slab and laid it across the opening; and then the other slab. Leah set Jim's turquoise nuggets in a row on top.

Geoffrey struggled into his father's pack, Leah into her daypack, and they started up the path. Chaco fell in behind them.

Chapter 24

Leah would never understand how it took only a few minutes to arrive at the cliff, which had taken her weeks to find.

"We can't climb it, Geoffrey. It's pitch black."

But instead of tackling the cliff, Geoffrey made a sharp left turn. He took her hand. Her feet magically found a narrow path. Minutes later, they were standing on top.

"How—?"

"That was the shortcut."

They surveyed the luminous sky, the black woods below. The cold breeze that had blown all evening suddenly died, and the fump-fump-fump of drums came. Leah's skin turned to gooseflesh.

Geoffrey tightened an arm around her waist. Chaco growled. The sound didn't float above the forest, but thumped up from the earth. Drums, and the faint chant of male voices, the wail of female voices. The ground vibrated like an engine. As they stood listening, the drumming faded and died.

Leah looked at Geoffrey in the moonlight. His face was old, far older than she thought he would ever be.

"Let's go," he said.

Geoffrey led at the steadfast pace he had used the last three days, the step of a man intimate with the forest and sure of his route. But when he spoke, his voice was small, like a frightened child's.

"What did he mean about Grandpa? What about the car?"

"I don't know. It almost sounded as if he saw him there."

"That doesn't make sense."

"No. It doesn't."

"There's no way Grandpa could find our car."

"Of course not. It's impossible."

"We have to go there."

"Yes, we do."

The detour to the car would cost valuable time, but they had no choice. They trudged along on mostly level ground now, still without a trail, but with some light from the stars and moon. Chaco stayed several yards ahead.

Geoffrey stopped. "If Jim hurt Grandpa…."

"If he did, what can we do about it? We already killed Jim."

"What?"

"Geoffrey, it's a joke. Remember jokes?"

"Huh."

"It was an awful joke. You don't have to laugh."

He walked on. Every few minutes, Chaco would double back and let the boy scratch his ears.

Now that they were so close to safety, Leah's mind raced. There were too many questions to ponder. She kept remembering the drums, the chanting; she kept seeing Jim's wracked body; she kept having tortured visions of BJ and Alissa despairing.

But then she felt her ancient friend walking beside her, calm as a stone. The woman said, "You've already survived death. What more is there to fear?"

She was right. Although her job was far from over, Leah was awake and alive.

"Geoffrey, wait a minute. What are we going to tell them?"

He stopped. "Who?"

"Everybody. The authorities. You know they won't let us walk away from this."

"Would they believe we just got lost?"

"What about your father? What about Howlin' Jim? What about Juana?"

He looked miserable. "We killed Jim. We're as much criminals as he was."

"But if we take them to the cavern…."

"We can't do that."

"No. We can't let them uncover the ancients. For your father's sake."

He walked more slowly.

"Geoffrey, can you lead them to Alissa and BJ on the east route?"

"I think so."

"Okay. There'll be a rescue party, a sheriff. We take them to camp on the east route. We won't tell them we came out from this end."

"Okay."

"There'll be a lot of questions. But you won't say anything unless I say it first, and you'll agree with me."

"Okay." He turned to hug her, then walked on.

"We're almost there." They entered a section of deep wood where the trees stood close together, the second growth after a long-ago forest fire. The branches intertwined, forming a roof that shut out the starlight.

"It's darker than the cave in here."

"Use the flashlight."

She lit their way over fallen timber, around rocks.

"Look there," said Geoffrey.

A boulder the size of a garage loomed before them. The light picked up something shiny.

"Our car!" Leah ran ahead of Geoffrey, tripping and fumbling in the dark.

They ran the beam over it. When she saw Alissa's little bike in the back, tears sprang into Leah's eyes. They opened the doors, saw their things inside. Nothing had been touched.

"Grandpa?" Geoffrey shouted. He got out from under his big pack, took the flashlight, and began to search in a circle. Leah leaned against Branson's side of the car.

Chaco let out a single bark. Geoffrey picked his way in that direction and tripped over a backpack. His grandfather was lying against it.

"Mom!"

The road was just a dirt Forest Service access, no asphalt. Leah's feet, unaccustomed to an even surface, stumbled as she took her first steps. She picked a direction and they started walking.

She and her son guided Geoffrey Ellis between them, his arms around their shoulders, his legs sometimes giving out and his head sometimes dropping as he passed in and out of consciousness.

A house-sized RV rumbled up behind them. It had a ladder up the back, aluminum chairs on top, and a license plate that read GIT SUM. A dead buck was strapped across the hood.

Geoffrey raised his hand, and the boxed monster ground to a halt. Two men with beer cans stepped down from the cab.

"Howdy, son," boomed the driver. "Who's that you got there?"

Geoffrey tried to smile, but his face was stuck. "It's my grandfather."

"He looks kinda done in."

"He's not used to being in the woods."

Leah stared hungrily at the deer, unable to talk.

"Kin we help you?"

"We've been lost."

"Lost? How kin ya get lost on the Rim? It's either up or down, ain't it?" The driver laughed.

"Hell, we tried to git lost," his buddy said. "Woulda loved to miss another day of work."

Leah shuddered as the cold wind whipped her hair against her cheek. Her jacket was full of holes, splattered with mud and blood. The driver stared at them.

"The old man's in pretty rocky condition, ain't he?"

"I think he'll be all right."

"You want a ride down the Rim, then?"

"Yes," she croaked. She couldn't look at the noisy man.

He walked them to the rear of the RV and turned the latch. "Guess you missed Thanksgiving," he said, as he offered Leah a hand up the metal step, then helped her get Mister Ellis stretched out onto a cot.

The camper was dark and warm, with parallel cots and a little stove and the smell of kerosene. Guns hung in racks; nylon carpeting felt spongy underfoot. Chaco leapt in and lay down.

"We're headed for Payson," the man said. "That okay?"

"That's fine."

"Anywhere particular in Payson?"

Mister Ellis raised his head. "Ranger station."

"Sure, but it's probably closed till Monday for the holiday."

Monday. Holiday. The words sounded foreign to Leah.

"Vern Crouse. Right next door."

"Okay, if it's a real emergency. His wife ain't too pleased when he gets called to work, his days off."

"It's an emergency," said Leah.

"Okay, we'll do 'er. You guys comfortable back here?"

"Yes. Thank you."

"There's sodas and potato chips in the cooler. You just help yourselves."

Leah stretched out on the other cot, and Geoffrey collapsed on the carpet between them. They listened to the door close. The big engine revved and the vehicle lurched forward. Leah lay on the soft, scratchy surface of the manmade blanket. Gradually her feet began to thaw.

Geoffrey reached up for her hand. "Mom? Have we got it all?"

"The story? Yes, I'm pretty sure. Just say what I say. Don't think any more, Geoffrey."

They were on their way to Payson, a town she'd heard of once. She had to sleep.

Mrs. Crouse cooked the turkey and all Vern's favorite dishes, substituting low-fat ingredients; then she set a pretty table with her grandmother's plates. Her son arrived from forestry school and started a blaze in the fireplace.

Vern came in from the shower, to mash the sweet potatoes and stir the gravy.

"Nothing from Jeff?"

He shook his head. "I hope he's okay."

"He's a careful man. Too bad he'll miss dinner, though."

"There'll be plenty of leftovers."

With no need to hurry, they lingered over supper. Vern and his son were scraping plates and cutting the pumpkin pie when they heard a vehicle in the driveway.

Mrs. Crouse rolled her eyes. "Well, we almost made it through a holiday meal without an interruption. Will you see who it is, Vern?"

Vern went to the front porch. "Howdy," he called.

The hunters opened the rear door of the RV. A dog bounded out.

The driver helped a bedraggled woman down the step and led her up the walk. She looked like a bag lady, scratched and dirty, with eyes that took in everything, though she moved stiffly. A freckle-faced boy followed. They stood under the porch light, staring at him.

"How can I help you folks?" said Vern.

Geoffrey Ellis stepped out of the RV, came slowly up the walk, and fell into Vern's arms.

❖ ❖ ❖ ❖ ❖

Vern did some basic tests and was pretty sure Mister Ellis didn't have a concussion—that he was just exhausted and dehydrated. The Crouses talked with him while Leah and Geoffrey wolfed their turkey, then offered to take a walk in the moonlight, to give the trio some privacy. Geoffrey Ellis sat on the sofa with Leah on one side, her head on his shoulder, and his grandson on the other side, staring at the floor.

"Branson's dead," was all Leah could say. She laid her hand in his palm.

He started to cry. "I know. I thought you all were."

"He fell off a cliff."

Geoffrey Ellis sat for a few moments. This account of his son's death was too sketchy. Perhaps Leah was telling it that way to protect his feelings. So he wouldn't picture his athletic, sure-footed son at the moment he died. But he did anyway; what did it matter?

He cleared his throat. "What about Alissa?"

"She's still there, with BJ."

"We'll go before daylight."

"How are you feeling?"

"I can drive."

There seemed nothing else to say tonight. He loaded them into his SUV. The boy fell asleep before his grandfather even got the doors closed.

On the way out the drive, his headlights picked out the Crouses, Vern walking with his arm around his wife, their son the future ranger stopping to examine some piñon bark.

Geoffrey Ellis waved through the windshield. They would understand why he left without a goodbye. He hoped Vern would give him some get-away time in the morning.

❖ ❖ ❖ ❖ ❖

Before dawn he left the motel for food at the All-Nite Mart. When he returned, Geoffrey was waiting for him, pink and warm from the shower. The boy—almost as tall as a man now—wrapped him in his strong, no-longer-boyish arms, and didn't release him until they were both laughing in disbelief at being together.

Leah came out into the dim morning. Her wet hair, once the color of fire, looked like straw; her face was haggard, her eyes too large. But she smiled and accepted the coffee he handed her.

"How's your head?"

"I'll be okay. Still a mystery what happened, though."

"Maybe you stood up under a branch and knocked yourself out."

"Maybe." He didn't believe it. But there were more important things to think about now.

Geoffrey directed his grandfather east, out of the sleeping town. Neither he nor Leah had been this way before, but he gave the directions with confidence, as if he'd been taking that route all his life.

Though he had many big questions, Geoffrey Ellis was learning to listen, not ask. If he waited, most answers would come to him.

"Your car was nowhere near here," he said, watching Geoffrey's face in the rear-view mirror. The boy's eyes darted toward his mother.

"No, it wasn't," Leah said.

"It was far to the west. Opposite direction."

"Yes."

He waited for an explanation.

"We left it there to throw people off," Leah said, looking out the window.

"You didn't want to be found."

"No."

"I see."

After a long silence, Leah said, "There was a girl with us. A local teenager."

Geoffrey Ellis thought, *Oh my god, the missing girl. What did Branson get them into?*

"She died," said Leah.

"She killed herself," said Geoffrey.

Geoffrey Ellis put his hand beneath his jacket, felt his heart.

"She killed herself," he said. "I see." He grasped the wheel and tried to concentrate on his driving. Geoffrey and Leah said nothing more. Finally Leah reached across and put her hand on his arm.

"We have a lot of explaining to do, don't we?"

He sighed heavily. "I'm afraid so."

"We haven't been ourselves."

"I see."

They drove a few miles along the top of the Rim before Geoffrey indicated the turnoff.

"We have to walk in, Grandpa. Maybe you should wait here."

"No way, boy. I'm in this, too."

Geoffrey led through the woods, with Mister Ellis following. Leah, bringing up the rear, had time to think about what else to tell her father-in-law. That ranger was probably on the phone with the sheriff right now. She'd better have some answers ready.

He found our car. He wasn't that far from our first camp. But even Leah, in all her days of searching, hadn't discovered the shortcut, the crack in the bowl. Chances were that he never would have found it, either.

Our story stands. The car was a decoy.

What about Juana? The truth would have to do. She couldn't change what Juana had done.

And what about Howlin' Jim?

Mister Ellis, stepping through the woods, called ahead to Geoffrey, "You're sure this is right."

"Positive."

"It's a long way from your car."

"Yeah." And Geoffrey continued, slipping along with such poise that even Leah almost believed he'd been there before.

After two hours they took a break, removing their packs and leaning against a log to rest. Leah's stomach, still reacting to the feast of the night before, could handle only small bites of the energy bars.

"The two of you move like Indians," Geoffrey Ellis said.

"We've been practicing."

"When I was searching for you in Phoenix, the name of Howlin' Jim turned up."

Here it comes, thought Leah. "Yes," she said.

He watched her face. "I take it this person had something to do with your decision to disappear."

Leah sighed. "He taught Branson a lot about the ancient people. It's humiliating how much influence he had over all of us. He convinced us to move up here. Then he abandoned us."

Geoffrey said, "We never saw Howlin' Jim again. After Dad died and Jim left, we came out."

"That's it? He left, and you came out?"

"Yes."

Leah and Geoffrey were both looking at him, straight in the eyes, as people are supposed to do when they're telling the truth. Maybe it was some version of the truth, but they'd left plenty out; that much he was sure of. It was as if they were challenging him—begging him—to buy it.

"I see," he said.

Chapter 25

When they reached familiar territory, Leah ran ahead. She thrashed through the brush, hardly feeling the poke of branches, the scrapes on her hands as she scrambled over rocks. *Please, please,* she prayed, and crept up on the camp, prepared to see something horrid.

BJ and Alissa huddled by the fire, roasting a magpie—and of all things, singing. Harmonizing on the chorus of "You Are My Sunshine." BJ spotted Leah and leapt up. Alissa, tears streaking the dirt and soot on her face, ran to hold onto her mother, the way a person tumbling over a cliff grasps at a branch.

Leah reached into her pack and thrust sandwiches at them. "Here. Eat."

BJ chomped the food so fast that she gagged. That made her cry, and laugh.

Leah held Alissa on her lap. "Grandpa's coming with Geoffrey," she said, and watched her daughter's expression of disbelief.

"Grandpa Geoffrey?"

"Yes. We're going out."

BJ, equally bewildered, said, "Where's Jim?"

"Don't know. Don't care. And you, BJ, don't even ask."

"But where—?"

"I said, don't ask."

BJ's eyes darted around, as if she'd just won a trip and couldn't decide what to pack.

Leah laughed. "Leave everything. You'll sleep in a bed tonight."

They were still staring at her when Geoffrey and his grandfather stepped into the campsite.

❖ ❖ ❖ ❖ ❖

For just a few moments, while her father-in-law and all her people were reunited in the grim camp, Leah forgot her weeks of despair. She glimpsed a future—one without Branson, but one in which she might see her children grow to adulthood.

Alissa, hardly believing her luck, leapt from mother to grandfather to brother, trying to hold all of them at once. They took turns hugging her and tousling her hair. She ran to her tent and gathered her treasures—twig dolls, pretty stones—and stuffed them into her little pack, ready to hike.

BJ was ashamed for Mister Ellis to see his former favorite vice-president starving, disillusioned, and clueless. But in her elation, she managed a wisecrack or two that reminded them she was still BJ.

They collected a few items to take, just clothing for the hike out. Leah told them to leave everything else as it was, because the sheriff would want to see.

"Sheriff?" said Alissa. "Are we criminals?"

"They'll want to understand about Juana."

"Will they dig her up?"

Leah sighed. In the past, in her distant, corrupt, civilized past, she would have tried to skim over the terrible details. But Alissa, like the rest of them, was now on a first-name basis with death—death of animals, of illusions, of people she loved.

"Yes, they probably will dig her up," Leah said. "I'm sure they will."

"What about Dad?"

"Dad's lost in the woods."

"But we know how to find him."

"He's lost, Alissa. He's not to be disturbed. Do you understand?"

"I guess."

"Repeat after me. We don't know where he is."

"We don't know where he is."

"Yes, it's a lie. I'm asking you to tell a lie. Will you do it?"

Alissa looked to her grandfather. He nodded. "Okay," she said.

"We'll come back some day for a visit. We know how to find him. But no one else does."

Leah had memorized the route. By nightfall, with only a few wrong turns, she and BJ and Alissa were at the edge of the Rim. From here they headed west to the SUV.

Geoffrey and his grandfather went to Branson's grave, where they sat listening to the wind. Geoffrey Ellis took it all in: the ponderosa, the talus, the stones covering his son's body at the bottom. He saw BJ's small deer of twig and adobe, Alissa's necklace of seed lodged in a crack, already half eaten by ground squirrels. He listened to the pop and clunk of rocks as they broke free of the cliff and bounced down to join the others.

He heard wind in the ponderosa, listened for spirit voices. He thought about his orchids under plastic in his greenhouse in Philadelphia, and wished he could leave his prized hybrid as an offering. He remembered Branson as a reckless child; Branson as a graceful, princely, rebellious, teen; Branson as a caged animal in the corporate offices of Ellis Equipment. He thought he heard voices and wondered why he'd never heard them before—if they'd always been there. His questions were dissolving, becoming part of the answers; the answers, part of the questions.

He would bring something for Branson, some day, when he understood better what his son would have wanted from him. For now, it was time to plunge back into the woods, to join his family at his car.

Alissa, running ahead along the edge of the Rim, spotted the SUV against the starry sky.

"Mom?"

"Get in, Liss. We'll wait for Grandpa and Geoffrey."

Alissa and BJ collapsed in the back seat. Leah got the heater going. The dashboard lights glowed red on their faces, and warmth filled the cozy interior like a campfire in a cave. Leah tuned the radio to a Navajo-language station. The soft tom-tom and flute, drifting over the air from Window Rock or Holbrook, filled her head as the ancients' drums had done the night before.

Her ancient friend was right: she had survived. What was there to fear now?

Of course it wasn't over. She would have to lead the sheriff back to examine the camp. She would have to face Juana's father, knowing she was sentencing him to live with her death for the rest of his life, just as she would.

There would be an investigation. To the questions they would ask, she would give the answers she chose, nothing more. What did she have to fear from questions?

Branson was lost, and he would stay lost. Leah was the leader of the tribe now. She had the power, maybe even the magic. She would let no one disturb Branson. The investigators could ask, but no one in her tribe—not BJ, Alissa, Geoffrey, or his grandfather—would reveal where he lay.

As for Howlin' Jim, he had abandoned them, and they decided to come out of the forest. They never saw him again. She repeated: "We never saw him again." She didn't even know his real name. No matter how many times and how many ways they asked, her story would not change.

The tom-tom music stopped, and a man's voice came on, speaking in soft, guttural Navajo that now sounded familiar, even though Leah didn't understand the words. She turned to look at BJ and Alissa, asleep in the back seat, their beautiful faces luminous. Innocence was still possible for them.

For herself and Geoffrey, they were forever linked by their loss, their knowledge, and their deed. Whenever they were together, Branson and Howlin' Jim would be with them. They might take up the habits of normal people and never talk about what they'd done, but their hearts would lie buried at the bottom of the cave.

Their secret was safe with the ancients.

Give the Gift of
WAKING THE ANCIENTS
to Your Friends and Colleagues

CHECK YOUR LEADING BOOKSTORE OR ORDER HERE

❑ **YES,** I want _____ copies of *Waking the Ancients: A Novel of the Mogollon Rim* at $14.00 each, plus $4.95 shipping per book. (Colorado residents please add .31 sales tax per book.) Canadian orders must be accompanied by a postal money order in U.S. funds. Allow 15 days for delivery.

My check or money order for $_____ is enclosed.

Name _____

Organization _____

Address _____

City/State/Zip _____

Phone_____ E-mail _____

Please make your check payable and return to:

Thundercloud Books
P.O. Box 97
Aspen, CO 81612

www.ThundercloudBooks.com